D0258093

004963701 0

# Bull's Eye Stage Coach

Marshal Dwight Stern and his posse are overseeing the loading of a shipment of gold onto a heavily armoured stage coach when they are ambushed in a surprise attack.

With Stern's fiancée held in the grip of one of the attackers and a double-barrelled shotgun pointing at her head, there's no time to play nice. With his hand on his gun and a prayer for the gunman to make a mistake and move the gun from Belinda's head, all he needs is a split second. . . .

# Bull's Eye Stage Coach

Billy Hall

**A Black Horse Western**

ROBERT HALE · LONDON

© Billy Hall 2013
First published in Great Britain 2013


ISBN 978-0-7198-0749-7

Robert Hale Limited
Clerkenwell House
Clerkenwell Green
London EC1R 0HT

www.halebooks.com

Typeset by
Derek Doyle & Associates, Shaw Heath
Printed and bound in Great Britain by
CPI Antony Rowe, Chippenham and Eastbourne

# CHAPTER 1

A chill ran down his back. His hand dropped to the butt of his holstered forty-five. His eyes darted to the door that led in from the street. There was nobody there.

He shivered suddenly, unexpectedly. An icy draft from nowhere ran down his spine. He frowned. His stomach tightened into a hard knot.

'Now what?' he muttered under his breath.

Dwight Stern was no stranger to the feeling. Trouble was about to erupt. He had no idea where it might come from. It would be soon, though. The feeling was familiar enough; by now he no longer doubted its ominous portent. He got up and walked to the small window, looking up and down the street. Nothing seemed out of place. He took a deep breath and returned to his desk.

He was certainly no stranger to trouble, either. It went with the job. Town marshal didn't sound like that big a deal. Town marshal in Headland, Wyoming Territory was a different matter.

It hadn't been that much of a job when he took the position. Then the big gold rush in the Black Hills, across the line in Dakota Territory, had hit. Just about the same time gold was also found in the hills close to Headland. It wasn't of the magnitude of the strikes around Lead and Deadwood, but it was sizeable. It changed everything.

He hated gold. A few struck it rich. Very few. A few more managed to scratch out day wages, digging or panning. Numberless more lost everything they had, searching for it. He wasn't sure who lost the most. The ones who failed in their quest often lost everything but their honor, their dignity, and their values. The ones who struck it rich usually lost the only things the 'losers' kept.

He took another deep breath and went back to the paperwork on his desk.

'Yeee haaaah!'

The exultant yell emanating from the Lucky Lady saloon down the street didn't so much as raise his eyebrows. It was the rapid series of gunshots following it that brought Dwight Stern to his feet.

He walked swiftly out the door, passing beneath the sign that announced Town Marshal, and strode toward the source of the sounds.

As he did his eyes swept up and down Headland's main street yet again. Nothing triggered any sense of alarm in his practiced gaze. It was just another day in an endless string of other days.

The sun was approaching the mountains, which raised their snowcapped peaks to the west of town. In

6

the clear, high air, they appeared almost near enough to touch. They were, in reality, more than thirty miles away.

The sun's angle did, however, put half of Headland's main street in shadow. Dwight availed himself of what little protection that shadow afforded as he proceeded toward the disturbance.

He already knew, with near certainty, what he would find. A large herd from the Mule Shoe ranch had been successfully driven to the railhead at Cheyenne about a week previous. Half the drovers had remained in Cheyenne. The cowboys who chose to stay on at the ranch had returned as a group early this morning. With several months' wages in their pockets, and just as many months' loneliness to make up for, they had stayed in town instead of returning at once to the ranch.

A stream of people spilled from the door of the Lucky Lady as Dwight approached. Clearly fleeing to safer space, they stopped as they saw him approach. They divided like water from the prow of a boat before him, allowing him unimpeded access to the saloon's door.

He stepped through the door and took a quick step to the side, his back against the front wall. His eyes adjusted to the darker interior almost instantly.

Near the far end of the bar, a boyish-looking cowhand stood spraddle-legged, a forty-five in his hand, waving it around randomly. A wide grin threatened the stability of both ears. He spotted Dwight immediately.

'Hey, Marshal!' he shouted. 'How ya doin'? I'm havin' a ball! I'm all wool an' a yard wide, an' I'm gonna get drunker'n a skunk.'

Although he was not conscious of having counted the shots he had heard, Dwight was well aware the young cowboy's gun was empty. He made no effort to reach for his own gun. Grinning broadly in a deliberate display of good-natured friendliness, he approached the young man.

'It looks to me like you got a pretty good start on that, all right,' he observed.

'I'm tyin' a good one on, that's for sure,' the cowpoke assured him.

'You bein' careful where you're shootin' that thing?' Stern asked.

'What thing?'

'That gun in your hand.'

The young man looked at the gun in his hand as if seeing it for the first time. He frowned in an effort to concentrate. He looked back at Dwight. 'Well, yeah. I just been shootin' it up in the air.'

'Yeah, but did you forget that you're inside? Up in the air, in here, means at the ceiling. But the ceiling's the floor upstairs. What happens if you shoot through the floor and hit someone upstairs?'

The cowboy frowned. He looked up at the ceiling, trying hard to comprehend what the marshal was saying.

'What's your name, son?' Stern asked him.

'Billy. Billy O'Leary. Best bronc wrangler on the Mule Shoe, at your service, Marshal. You got any bad guys you need help handlin'? I'll sure's shootin' take care of 'em for ya.'

'Well, Billy, why don't you let me take care of that gun for you, while you manage to drink up your wages. That way you can get just as drunk as you want to, and nobody'll accidently get hurt.'

Billy frowned at him for a long moment. 'You gonna give it back to me when I get sobered up?'

'Sure. I just don't want you doin' somethin' you'll regret later.'

Billy thought about it a moment, then holstered the gun. He missed the holster twice before he succeeded in getting it put away. Then he unbuckled his gunbelt and handed it to the marshal. 'You're a good man, Marshal,' he said for no apparent reason.

Dwight took the gunbelt in his left hand, then addressed several cowboys sitting at two tables in the general vicinity. 'Are you boys with Billy?'

Several of them nodded wordlessly.

'Any of you stayin' sober enough to keep your friend from gettin' rolled or killed?'

An older man whose face was etched by wind and sun nodded. 'I'm sorta keepin' an eye on the boys. I got most o' their money squirreled away for 'em. Billy's gun was empty by the time you got here, you know.'

Dwight nodded. 'Yeah.'

He scanned the faces of the rest of the Mule Shoe crew. Within a couple weeks they would all return to work with splitting headaches, empty pockets, and more than likely some lingering 'souvenirs' from the

9

'soiled doves' who would, by then, be in possession of most of their money.

That routine of the range was of little concern to Stern. Of greater concern was the danger of someone getting in the way of a drunk cowboy intent on shooting holes in the ceiling. Either that, or shooting out a lamp, with a resulting fire that could wipe out half the town.

'You handled that plumb good, Marshal.'

Dwight nodded at a hand he recognized from the Flying Vee spread. 'Aw, he's just a kid that didn't mean any harm,' he said. 'No sense gettin' too excited.'

'Yeah, as long as he don't go doin' it down at the Golden Nugget.'

'Yeah, that might be a problem,' Dwight agreed.

The words called up his ongoing concern of the likelihood of a clash between one of those cowboys and an equally inebriated miner from one of the gold mines that were now scattered about the area.

That wasn't usually a major problem. The cowboys and ranchers mostly frequented the Lucky Lady saloon, while the miners generally favored the Golden Nugget saloon, a block down the street. Mule-skinners, bull-whackers, soldiers, and what few homesteaders there were, just about evenly split their business, patronizing whichever of the establishments struck their fancy at the time.

After another glance around the saloon, he left by the front door. Most of those who had fled the random shooting were already back inside, acting as if nothing out of the ordinary had happened.

Dwight looked right and left, up and down the street. Most of his time and effort, with the exception of the occasional serious crime, was taken up by the two saloons.

Of the two, he much preferred the Lucky Lady. Cowboys were generally boisterous, impulsive, and often violent. They usually managed to get very drunk when they came to town. They were ready to fight each other, or anyone else for that matter, at the drop of a hat. But beneath that, their nature was mostly good-hearted and even sentimental. The miners, on the other hand, tended to be of a much more sour disposition, often bitter, morose, even cruel. He attributed it to the difference between life in the sun and life spent mostly underground, but he didn't know if there was any substance to that supposition.

At the end of the main street a more elaborate and pretentious Pastime Emporium catered to the higher class of citizen. It was the only establishment of its kind Dwight had ever known to be operated by a woman. Belle Le Beaux ran it with an iron hand. Her 'girls' were refined enough that they actually patronized the town's businesses that didn't welcome the 'horizontal workers' of the other two saloons. Nobody got out of line at the Pastime. It was rumored that the 'girls' who worked as bouncers there could put the toughest man in town on his back in a heartbeat, and have him begging for mercy.

That there was some truth to the rumor was

reflected in the fact that Dwight had never once needed to set foot inside the place since it had opened nearly two years previous.

His reverie was shattered as his eyes lit on the man leaning against a post that supported the awning in front of the saddle shop. Alarm bells sounded in his mind instantly. The man had neither moved nor spoken, but Dwight immediately recognized him as a threat. Without consciously looking at it, he noticed the man wore a tied-down Smith & Wesson forty-four with a five inch barrel. He was also willing to bet that the front sight had been filed off, to be sure it didn't interfere with a quick draw.

The man returned his stare without expression. His gaze was cold and hard. It reminded Dwight of looking into the eyes of a rattlesnake.

'You always look for awkward young kids to embarrass like that?' the man demanded.

The hackles rose on the back of Dwight's neck. It might have been an innocent enough remark, if it had been made by someone else, or in a different tone, or by someone with a legitimate interest in the cowboy's feelings. To Dwight, it was a clear challenge.

His voice was soft, but his eyes returned the hard gaze of the stranger. 'Why would that be any business of yours?' he asked.

'I just hate to see some young kid made to look like a fool just so a lawman can make himself out to be a tough guy,' the man asserted.

'Your concern's real touching.' Dwight grinned, attempting to defuse the situation.

The man was having none of that. 'I bet you ain't so tough with them as is already dry behind the ears.'

'I don't remember you,' the marshal said, instead of answering the man's challenge. 'You new in town?'

'Now I don't see as that's any o' your business.'

'You're wrong on that one. That is my business. I'm the marshal. You new in town?' he demanded again.

The man straightened from leaning on the post. His hand brushed the handle of the Smith & Wesson on his hip, polished from countless contacts with his hand. 'And I say that ain't none o' your business. Why don't you try takin' my gun away from me, like you did that kid.'

'If I have to, I will,' Dwight assured him.

That was all the man was waiting for. His gun fairly leaped into his hand, lifting to center on the star on Dwight's vest.

Fast as the man was, Dwight was both ready and faster. His Colt blasted an instant ahead of the stranger's Smith & Wesson. The man was slammed backward by the force of the bullet. His own shot, a split second later, went wide and high, soaring harmlessly into the distance.

The man staggered a step backward, fighting to maintain his balance. He frowned quizzically, trying to grasp what had happened. He fought to bring his gun to bear on the marshal, but it seemed suddenly much heavier than normal. It sagged downward. He squeezed the trigger, and it fired into the ground. The recoil jerked it out of his grip. It landed in the dusty street. He followed it a second later, his eyes wide, staring without blinking and without sight at the dust that suddenly covered his eyes.

Dwight frowned as he holstered his Colt.

'What happened, Marshal?' a slightly overweight man with mutton-chop sideburns demanded.

Dwight sighed. 'Fella called me out, just plumb outa the blue. Made himself an excuse to draw on me. You know him, Walt?'

Walter Newsome, editor of the *Headland Courier*, shook his head. 'I have not had the pleasure of the gentleman's company,' he replied.

'You're no help,' Dwight complained. 'I thought you newspaper guys knew everything.'

Walt chuckled. 'It only seems that way because we are always incredibly well-informed, and because we are so uncannily intelligent.'

'Yeah, that's it all right,' Dwight responded.

A crowd had already gathered. He felt a sudden need to escape the barrage of questions sure to be directed at him. 'Holler at Corny for me, would you, Walt?'

Without waiting for the newspaperman to answer, he headed up the street toward his office. Cornelius Janderslaag was the undertaker. He'd take care of the stranger's body. He would also duly bill the town for doing so. He guessed that was fair enough.

The premonition of danger should have dissipated with the stranger's death. It didn't. Its chills continued to play that icy tune of terror up and down his spine.

14

# CHAPTER 2

' 'Scuse me, Marshal.'

Dwight looked the young man up and down. He seemed to bear no threat. He was average height, maybe five-foot-seven, muscular, at close to 150 pounds, tousled brown hair jutting from beneath a slightly smaller hat than cowboys wore. Clear brown eyes met Dwight's with neither timidity nor challenge.

'What can I do for you?' the marshal replied.

'Just wondered if you might know somebody in town that's hirin',' the man said. 'I'm sorta in need of a job.'

'Didn't strike it rich, huh?'

He grinned. 'Didn't try. Trompin' around the hills turnin' rocks over ain't never struck me as a good way to make a livin'.'

'What do you do for a livin'?'

'Whatever's available. Work with my hands. I'm pretty handy. I'm stout. I'm a good worker.'

'What's your name?'

15

'Goode. Lester Goode.'

'Where you from, Lester?'

'Just Les, if you don't mind. Missouri.'

Dwight grinned. 'Les Goode. I 'spect you get a bad time about that now and then.'

Les grinned in response. 'I've been ribbed about worse stuff than my name.'

'You ever do any carpenterin'?'

'Yeah. Quite a little, as a matter o' fact.'

'You any good at it?'

'More'n just good. I've been told I drive nails like lightnin'.'

'That so?'

'Yup. My hammer never strikes twice in the same spot.'

Dwight chuckled. 'Makes it kinda hard to get a nail driven, don't it?'

'Naw. It just takes a little longer. But havin' to swing the hammer twice as much makes my arm stronger. Actually, I ain't really all that bad.'

'Well, Virgil Zucher's lookin' for a man or two. He's got more work than he can handle, what with all the buildin' goin' on.'

'The town does seem right prosperous. Where could I find Mr Zucher?'

'You won't find him at all if you call 'im "Mr Zucher". He'll just tell you Mr Zucher was killed in the war.'

The stranger frowned. 'Why would he say that?'

' 'Cause his father was killed in the war.'

Goode grinned. 'Oh. Well, then, where could I

find Virgil?'

Dwight pointed at one of the streets running at rightangles to the main street. 'His house is up that street. It'd be the fifth house, I guess. He's got a shingle out front, so you can't miss it. He's more'n likely over at the bank now, though.'

'The bank?'

'The Headland Land and Mineral Bank, not the other one. They're startin' to build on. They're gonna more'n double the size of the bank.'

'That oughta be a good sized job. Banks build right good. "Hell for stout", as the sayin' goes.'

'Makes folks feel like their money's secure, that way.'

'There's a lot o' money in the banks in this town, I'm bettin'.'

'Why's that?'

'Well, it's good cow country, an' beef's pertneart six cents a pound, I hear, so the ranchers gotta be doin' good. Then there's all the gold comin' outa the hills. Lots o' people flockin' inta the area means the merchants are makin' money hand over fist. Yup, the banks oughta be plumb full o' money.'

Something about the way he said it excited a brief flurry of activity by the spine chills that had been troubling Dwight, but the sensation disappeared almost as soon as it started.

'There's just the two banks,' Dwight said absently. 'Wells Fargo and Headland Land and Mineral Bank.'

'The stage line belongs to Wells Fargo too, I noticed,' Les observed.

17

'Yeah. They could likely use a good man or two as well.'

'The bank?'

'No, the stage line. It's run separate from the bank. They've been runnin' kinda short on drivers and guards lately.'

'Oh. Well, I guess I'll see about the carpenter thing first. Drivers and guards on the stagecoach have a way of becoming targets too often for my taste.'

Their conversation was interrupted by a cowboy, whose gait was far from steady. 'Hey, you! Marshal!'

Dwight turned to face the man, as Goode waved nonchalantly and sauntered away. 'What can I do for you?'

The man's voice was slurred but his response was instant. 'You can give my friend his gun back, that's what you can do.'

'Who's your friend?'

'Billy O'Leary, that's who.'

Dwight nodded. 'Well, I'll be plumb happy to give him his gun back when he's sobered up and ready to head out to the ranch.'

'He don' wanna wait. He's wantin' 'is gun back now.'

'Well, I don't think that's too good an idea. He's apt to get himself in a whole batch of trouble if he has it while he's workin' on drinkin' up his wages.'

'I don' really care what you think. I think he oughta have his gun back now. I come to make you give it back to 'im.'

18

'You're Harley Jensen, aren't you?'

'Yes I am. An' you're Marshal Dwight Stern. See, I know who you are too. An' Billy O'Leary's my friend. An' you're gonna give me Billy O'Leary's gun, so I can take it back to him.'

'No, I guess that's what I'm not going to do,' Dwight disagreed. 'And while we're on the subject, I have an idea you oughta let me keep your gun too. That way you and Billy can both get just as drunk as you want to get, without either one of you getting in trouble.'

The young cowboy's drunkenness seemed to diminish instantly. His eyes remained bleary and watery, but his stance straightened. His hand dropped to the butt of his gun. His voice was stronger and steadier as he said, 'You ain't takin' my gun.'

'If you don't give it to me, I'll have to take it.'

Harley jerked his gun from its holster with startling speed, considering his obviously inebriated state. Even sober, however, his draw would have been much too slow. He was all cowboy, not a gunfighter. He wore a gun to use on any rattlesnakes he saw, on mad cows if he was cornered, and for self-defense if necessary. It was more of a tool of his trade than it was a weapon in his hands.

In a blur of speed, Dwight swept his own gun from its holster and slammed it into the side of the cowboy's head. Jensen dropped his own gun and fell sideways on to the board sidewalk. He immediately began to struggle to stand up.

19

Whether from the amount of whiskey he had consumed or the effect of the blow to his temple, or both, he had a great deal of difficulty doing so. With a monumental effort he fought his way to his feet. 'You hit me,' he mumbled accusingly.

Dwight nodded. His own gun was back in its holster. The cowboy's gun was already safely tucked into his waistband. 'Yeah, I did. I for sure didn't want to have to shoot you.'

The cowboy shook his head in an effort to clear the cobwebs. It was the wrong thing to do. Instead of clearing it, it resulted in greater dizziness. He fell back against the front of the store they stood before. His eyes slowly focused again. 'You gonna lock me up?' he asked.

Dwight shook his head. 'No, I'll just hang on to your gun till you're ready to head outa town. Stop by then and I'll give it back to you.'

'You couldn'ta done that, if'n I was sober.'

'I wouldn't have needed to, if you were sober.'

'Do you know Doxy?'

'Doxy? Who's Doxy?'

'She's one o' the girls at the Lucky Lady. The redhead. She's one fine woman, Doxy is. I think I'll go talk to Doxy for a while.'

'Why don't you do that,' Dwight encouraged.

With an effort Harley pushed himself away from the wall that supported him. His knees far from steady and his feet too widely placed, he nonetheless began to pick up momentum as he headed back down the street toward the Lucky Lady.

20

'Herdin' drunks, hazin' drifters, an' facin' down gunslingers,' Dwight muttered as he headed down the street. 'There's gotta be a better way to make a livin'.'

As he continued along the street toward his office he walked toward the front of Lowenberg's Mercantile Store. He took hold of one of the posts supporting the wooden awning, and stepped up on to the board sidewalk. His gaze habitually swept the length of the street. Just then a flash of sunlight caught his eye. He jerked his head toward it, hand dropping to his gun. Even as he did, he heard the unmistakable 'thunk' of a bullet burying itself in the post beside his head.

He dived to the board sidewalk and rolled, as the 'thunk' of a second bullet hit the outside wall of the store. He continued the roll, coming up on one knee, gun in hand. He snapped off a quick shot at the space between two stores on the opposite side of the street, the spot where he had seen the sun flashing on gun metal.

Some part of his mind heard yet another gun fire off to his left.

He sprang up and slid backward into the space between Lowenberg's Mercantile Store and Glendenning's Hardware. The street was suddenly as still as death. What pedestrians were on the street were pressed back against the walls of whatever business they were in front of. Most had hurriedly ducked into the nearest doorway, and were peering warily out.

21

Dwight left his cover and ran directly across the street, watching the space from which he was sure the shots had come. There was no sign of anyone there now.

Across the street, he hugged the store front and approached the space marked by the brief flash of sunlight. Removing his hat, he thrust his head out and back again swiftly. He studied the picture in his mind that that instantaneous glimpse had provided. Squatting down, he repeated the maneuver, his head no more than two feet above the ground. This time he left his head exposed an instant longer, to allow himself a better look.

There was nothing there.

Stepping cautiously into the space between the buildings, he moved to the back of the stores. There was nothing in sight but weeds, empty space, and a scattering of windblown trash.

He walked back to the front of the stores. He studied the sides of the building. He found where his bullet had buried itself in the cedar siding. Three inches in front of it another furrow was plowed into the siding.

'I thought I heard somebody else shootin',' he muttered.

He holstered his gun and pulled out his knife. He dug into the cedar board just beyond the end of the furrow that marked that other bullet's path. He was rewarded by a flattened piece of lead. He held it in his hand, studying it with a puzzled expression.

'Smaller'n a forty-five or forty-four, either one,' he

22

mused. 'Now who in Sam Hill carries a smaller handgun that'd be shootin' at a guy that was shootin' at me?'

'Are you OK, Marshal?'

Dwight looked up at David Lowenberg, aware for the first time that the store owner had followed him across the street. He noted approvingly that the merchant carried a double-barreled shotgun. 'Yeah, thanks, Dave,' he responded. 'Someone took a potshot at me.'

'I heard the shots. Two from over here, then I thought I heard you shoot back, then I saw you runnin' over here. I thought I'd see if you needed a hand.'

'Did you hear any other shots?'

'Other shots?'

'Yeah. I thought I heard someone else shoot once.'

Lowenberg frowned in deep thought for a long moment. 'No, I can't rightly say I did. Of course I was busy grabbin' my shotgun to see what was goin' on, so I mighta just not heard it. What is goin' on?'

'I don't know, Dave. I don't know. I don't like it, though; I can tell you that.'

'Gossip has it that fella you shot the other day seems to've come into town just to call you out.'

'Acted that way, all right.'

'Someone out to get you?'

It was obvious that somebody was. More than one somebody. That knot in the pit of his stomach was getting bigger by the day. Twice in recent days he was the obvious target of somebody. Who wanted to get rid of him that badly? Why? If it was some personal grudge, it would have ended with the death of the first man who confronted him. That just wasn't the case. He had never met that man before.

Now someone had tried to gun him down in cold blood from hiding. Was it someone who hated him for some reason, or someone hired to do the job? If he was hired to do it, by whom? And why? Why would it suddenly be that important for anyone to get rid of a small town marshal?

Whatever it was, he wouldn't be long in coming, he was sure of that.

# CHAPTER 3

'My, my! You are one pretty little filly. However did a girl as pretty as you manage to be stuck in a crude slap-dabble town like this?'

'I beg your pardon,' Belinda Holdridge mumbled, moving to go around the man standing in her way.

Instead of allowing her to pass the man moved closer, blocking her way more effectively. 'Aw, now, that's no way to treat a lonesome gentleman,' he remonstrated. 'You could at the very least afford me a few minutes of polite conversation.'

Put off by his forwardness, but simultaneously intrigued by his smooth speech and flawless English, Belinda hesitated. 'I'm sorry. I am not in the habit of visiting with strangers on the street.'

'Well now,' the man responded, 'that's commendable. But on the other hand, who do you know that didn't start out being a stranger to you? Aside from my parents, every friend I have used to be a stranger.'

She looked directly at him for the first time. His eyes were bright and clear. He was plainly not intoxicated. A slight smile played at the corners of his mouth, but his look was neither taunting nor threatening.

She almost stammered as she said, 'But at least they were all introduced to me by somebody. I don't believe we have been introduced.'

The man swept off his hat, stepped to one side, and motioned to the spot he had been standing. 'In that case, Madam, may I introduce you to Mr Jarvis McCrae, presently of Headland, Wyoming Territory.'

Then he stepped back into the spot he had so recently vacated and extended his right hand, while still holding his hat in his left. 'Why thank you, sir. And to whom, may I ask, have I just this moment been introduced?'

Belinda giggled in spite of her best effort to remain stern. 'M-My name is Belinda Holdridge, Mr McCrae.'

In spite of the fact that she had not extended her own hand, he reached out and grabbed her right hand. Instead of shaking it, as was the custom for both men and women in that country, he simply lifted her hand slightly and bowed over it. For the barest moment she actually thought he was going to kiss her hand. Then she wasn't sure whether she hoped he would or wouldn't. She drew her hand back from his, knowing she had turned bright red.

'Is that Miss Belinda Holdridge?' he asked, ignoring the fact that she had jerked her hand away from him.

'As if it were any of your business, yes, it is Miss Holdridge. If it were any of your business, I would also tell you that I am engaged to be married. Now please stand aside and let me pass.'

Still holding his hat in his hand, he stepped to the very outer edge of the board sidewalk, bowed deeply with a sweep of his hat in the direction she had been trying to go. 'Of course, Miss Belinda Holdridge. It has been such a pleasure meeting you. I do hope I will have the pleasure of more of your charming company in the near future.'

Unsure how to respond, she said nothing. She walked on past, and he did nothing to impede her passing. A few steps later she glanced back over her shoulder. He was standing there smiling, obviously waiting for her to turn. As she did, he lifted his hat to her again.

She whirled back in the other direction and collided with Hildagarde Swenson, who was just exiting Lowenberg's Mercantile Store with a bag of merchandise.

'Oh! Oh, my! Oh, I'm so sorry, Mrs Swenson! I . . . I'm afraid I wasn't watching where I was going. Are you all right?'

'Oh, of course, my dear,' Mrs Swenson replied. 'I've been run into harder than that by one or another of my children every day of the week.'

As she answered she looked back over Belinda's shoulder at McCrae, who was grinning broadly. 'Is that a friend of yours?' she asked, her voice almost accusatory.

'Oh, no! No. He just . . . just . . . well, I'm not really sure what he just did.'

27

'Whatever do you mean? Did he bother you?'

'No! Yes. No. Not really. He . . . he just, sort of stopped me as I was walking by. He managed to introduce himself to me and to ask my name, and . . . and, well I'm afraid I was just a little bit flustered.'

'Why, how forward of him!' Hildagarde huffed. 'A lady can't even walk down the sidewalk these days without being accosted by some ruffian.'

'Oh, I don't think he is that,' Belinda protested. 'He . . . he talks like he's very sophisticated.'

'Hmmph! If he had any measure of sophistication he certainly wouldn't be causing sidewalk collisions between respectable ladies.'

'I think he must be new in town.'

'Hmmph! Half of the people on the street are new in town these days. Why, one hardly knows whom to speak to and whom to avoid. You must mention the incident to Dwight. I'm sure he will have more than just a passing interest in a stranger who accosts his betrothed on a public sidewalk.'

Belinda almost giggled at the self-righteous umbrage that was so incongruent in such a raw and often crude place. She managed to conceal her feelings, however. 'Well, I apologize again for almost knocking you down, Hilda. I am, as a matter of fact, just on my way to Dwight's office. He's taking me to supper tonight.'

Hildagarde brightened at once. 'Oh, how nice! You'll be eating at Sven and Helga's?'

'Uh, no, I think he mentioned being hungry for something that Ling Xao makes.'

Hildagarde's visage darkened instantly. 'Oh. I see. I much prefer good American food, myself.'

Belinda couldn't resist the urge to say, 'Yes, like lutefisk and lefse.'

Hildagarde missed the sarcasm entirely. 'Oh, my, yes. Exactly. So much better than those foreign foods, made out of goodness knows what. Well, I must be going. Please do say hello to Dwight for Soren and me.'

Before she told Dwight anything else, Belinda related her conversation about the competing eating establishments, and Hildagarde's failure to grasp her almost snide humor. He laughed aloud at the picture.

Then Belinda told him the reason for her near collision with Hildagarde, and his visage darkened instantly. 'Did he bother you? Did he touch you? I'll beat him within an inch of his life!'

She laid a hand on his arm. 'Oh, darling, don't be so protective! Of course he didn't touch me. He only wanted to wrangle an introduction.'

'Did you let him know you was taken?'

'Taken?' she asked, arching her eyebrows. 'Taken? You mean as if you lined up the eligible women in Headland and said, 'I'll take that one,' like you were picking out a heifer for a herd of cows?'

'You know what I mean,' he replied, growing angry because he knew his face was suddenly red. 'Did you tell him you and me are engaged?'

'Why, darling, I do believe you are blushing! Yes, dear. I made sure to tell him I was engaged to be

29

married. I did not tell him that if the man I am engaged to doesn't get around to making a married woman out of me pretty shortly, I may well change my mind, however.'

He gaped at her as if he couldn't believe she had said such a thing. 'But . . . but . . . but we agreed that we needed a place to live an' all that, afore we went an' tied the knot.'

'And just what do you call your house? Isn't that a place to live?'

'Well, yeah, but . . . but . . . well, there's some things I been savin' up for, that I really wanted to have in the house afore I went an' asked you to go ahead an' marry me an' start livin' there.'

She giggled at his discomfiture. 'Stop stammering, dear. I know exactly what you are doing. But I am getting tired of waiting. I want to be your wife. I want to have children. I'm not getting any younger, you know.'

At a loss for an adequate answer, he opened and closed his mouth a couple times, then changed the subject completely. 'I . . . had another guy shoot at me today.'

'Oh dear! Another one? I didn't even hear about it. What happened?'

He took a deep breath. 'Plumb outa nowhere. Tried to bushwhack me from between a couple build-ings. I caught a flash o' sun off'n his gun barrel just afore he shot. I took a dive an' he missed. I shot back, but I was just shootin' blind into the space he was in. Didn't hit 'im. It seemed almost like somebody'd sent 'im into town just to get rid o' me.'

'Oh, dear!' Belinda said again. 'Oh, dear! That's what you thought about the man you had to shoot the other day, too. Why ever would somebody do that?'

He frowned. 'Danged if I know. Worries me, though. He showed up just after this other fella shows up an' comes to me askin' where he might find a job. Most folks never think o' asking the marshal about jobs. Then this other fella bothers you. You said he was a stranger in town, too? What did he look like, anyhow?'

'He's about your height, maybe an inch or two shorter. Brown hair. Brown eyes. Wears a hat that's sorta different from most.'

Dwight's eyes widened. 'Sorta small for a Stetson, but bigger'n a bowler or a derby?'

'Yes. Do you know him?'

Instead of answering, Dwight said, 'Does he talk kinda highfalutin'. Real proper English and all that?'

'Yes. You do know him.'

Dwight frowned. 'That's another guy that came to me to ask about findin' work, oh, maybe a week ago. Jarvis McCrae, I think his name is.'

It was her eyes' turn to widen. 'You don't suppose there's some connection between his talking to you and his talking to me, do you?'

He said nothing for a long moment. She could not figure out the direction of his thoughts. She frowned. 'Is there something happening in town that you're not telling me about?'

31

He took a deep breath. 'Nothin' that I can talk about.'

She opened her mouth to reply, then shut it again. Abruptly he said, 'Let's go over to Ling's and see if he's got any lutefisk.'

Belinda giggled. 'Ugh. I tasted that stuff once. Once is enough.'

'I never got past the smell, myself.'

Arm in arm they left the marshal's office and headed for the café. The niggling little worry that kept turning over in the back of Dwight's mind had Lester Goode on one side of it and Jarvis McCrae on the other side of it. Part of the worry was wondering why either man worried him. He had a strong hunch he would know before long.

# CHAPTER 4

Hammers and saws produced a constant cacophony of busy sounds. Customers at Headland Land & Mineral Bank had to virtually shout at the tellers to make themselves heard. The tellers, in turn, leaned forward almost against the bars of their 'cages' to hear. It was a difficult environment in which to do business.

Bank president Hiram Birdwell kept a throw rug against the bottom of his office door, where there was a gap between door and floor. It not only kept out some of the sawdust and dirt of the ongoing construction, it helped to muffle the sound.

He and Oliver Standish, President of High Country Mining Enterprises, struggled to keep their voices low enough to avoid being overheard, yet loud enough to clearly understand one another.

'Can you assure me the shipments from here to Cheyenne will be completely safe?' Standish demanded.

Birdwell leaned back in his leather chair, folded

his hands across his ample stomach, and nodded effusively enough to make his mutton-chop whiskers bounce on his rotund face. 'Oh, absolutely, Mr Standish. Absolutely.'

He leaned forward, lowered his voice conspiratorially. 'In fact, as of three weeks from today, we will have the most safe and secure conveyance of valuables ever to be seen in this country.'

Standish's eyebrows rose inquisitively. 'And what, may I ask, is that?'

Because Birdwell's voice dropped even further, the mining executive had to lean forward, until their heads almost touched, to hear. 'Have you heard of the armored stagecoach that has just recently been put into use over at Deadwood and Lead?'

Standish only nodded.

'That same company – Concord Stages – has made more than one of those conveyances. Our own Wells Fargo company, that services this community, has purchased a second one just like it, for use in transporting our assets to Cheyenne.'

Standish pursed his lips. 'How safe is it?'

'It is strictly state of the art,' Birdwell assured him. 'There is a large strongbox anchored to the top of the coach itself. It is made of hardened steel. It is secured with not one, not two, but three heavy, hardened steel hasps, and padlocked with locks that cannot be jimmied, pried opened, or cut. In fact, a bullet from a thirty-thirty or forty-four-forty, either one, fired from a distance of only fifty feet, either bounces off or just flattens into a mass of lead,

34

without damaging the lock in any way.'

'Can't they just take the whole strongbox and work on it someplace at leisure?'

Birdwell shook his head. 'Not a chance. The box itself is firmly anchored to a sheet of steel, just as impervious to any tool, that covers the entire top of the stagecoach. All in all it weighs more than half a ton. Even if someone could remove it from the rest of the stagecoach, it is so large and cumbersome, as well as heavy, as to be impossible to convey.'

Standish pursed his lips in concentration again. 'Well, it sounds pretty secure.'

Birdwell bobbed his head enthusiastically. 'It is that, but just to make it even more secure, every shipment includes the usual armed driver and shotgun guard, plus two armed guards inside the coach, plus four outriders, maintaining a distance of two hundred yards before and behind the stage itself at all times. It would take a crack military unit even to approach it, and if anyone did manage to do so, they would find themselves helpless to avail themselves of any of the valuables entrusted to it.'

'But couldn't those guards be shot by, say, some men in the cover of the timber where the road passes through such places?'

Birdwell grinned as he responded. 'Not likely. Remember the outriders. They'd be sure to spot anyone positioned to do that. Besides, I hadn't mentioned that the sides of the coach also have iron plates on both sides of the coach. They have cross shaped openings through which the inside guards can shoot, but bullets from outside won't penetrate the sides of the coach.'

Standish whistled. 'That thing has to be prohibitively heavy.'

'It is heavy. It takes an eight-horse team, instead of the usual four or six, and it doesn't travel as fast as a normal stagecoach, but it is certainly secure.'

A long period of silence ensued, as each man leaned back in his chair, lost in thought. Finally Birdwell said, 'What are you thinking, Oliver?'

Standish smiled. 'Actually I was trying to think like a highwayman. What would I do, if I really wanted the cargo that was being shipped in that manner?'

'And what would you do?'

'I don't know. That's what delights me. Once the gold is placed in that strongbox and locked down, and the guards are in place, I can't think of a way to get at it.'

'I believe that's a fair assessment.'

'When did you say that coach is arriving?'

'It won't be here until just about three weeks from now.'

Oliver pondered that information with a contemplative frown. 'We haven't shipped out any gold for well over a week. If we wait three more weeks, we'll be putting five or six weeks' worth of production from the mine in one shipment. The gold alone will weigh close to a thousand pounds.'

'It will, indeed, be an awfully large shipment. But worth the wait to know it will be secure.'

Seemingly satisfied, Standish rose to leave.

Birdwell hurried to the office door and removed the rug from the bottom. He failed to notice that something had been slid under the door, and that the rug had been pushed to one side, leaving an opening through which sound could travel. Neither was he able to see Les Goode leave the piece of wood trim he seemed to be working on, just beside the door on its other side, and move to a different task.

# CHAPTER 5

'Howdy, Walt. I didn't expect to see you out an' about today. Ain't this the day you're usually elbow deep in ink?'

Walt Newsome flashed Dwight an unaccustomed grin. 'Good afternoon, Marshal. Yes, as a matter of fact, I usually am. Not today, however.'

'No newspaper this week?'

'Oh my, yes. Yes indeed. The *Headland Courier* will be issued promptly on time, as always.'

Dwight cocked his head to one side, a hint of a smile playing at the corners of his mouth. 'What'd you do – write this week's news last week?'

Walt chuckled. 'Not hardly. It would be convenient to be that prescient, to be sure, but I'm afraid I'm not. No, I finally had a circumstance of great fortune. I hired a pressman who actually knows what he's doing.'

'Is that so? How'd you happen to find him?'

Walt shrugged. 'Just one of those random vagaries of fortune, I presume. He simply came strolling into the newspaper office one day and asked if I had any need for an experienced typesetter. I was, as you said, elbow deep in ink at the time and pushing like the devil to get things done on time, so I hired him. He jumped right in, as if he had been on the payroll a long while. He set type faster than anybody I have ever seen. Excepting myself, of course. Then he went right about setting up the press as if he had been doing it for years.'

'Wow! I'd guess that doesn't happen very often in your line of work.'

'You have most certainly gotten that right! It has never, ever happened to me before. But please understand I am not complaining.'

'What's his name?'

'Mac. Well, his name is Jarvis McCrae, but he just goes by Mac.'

Dwight's expression became markedly more serious. 'When did all this happen?'

'Oh, nigh on to three weeks ago.'

'Hmm.'

'What do you mean, "Hmm?" That sounds like something ominous, the way you said it.'

Dwight shook his head. 'Yeah, well, I've already heard about this guy. He stopped Belinda on the sidewalk the other day. Wrangled himself an intro-duction that made her plumb uncomfortable.'

'Did he offend her?'

Dwight shook his head. 'Naw, not really. Just seemed pretty forward. Backed off when she told him she was promised.'

'Well, then, I don't see what the problem is.'

'It just seems like a strange coincidence. That'd be just almost the same time another new guy in town came along lookin' for a job. He hired on with Virgil. Virgil says he's one o' the best carpenters he's ever hired. Then this guy hires on with you. Then there's that new guy I heard about at Glendenning's Hardware store. Another well-educated guy, it sounds like. I ain't met him yet, though.'

'You don't say. A veritable outpouring of qualified laborers fortuitously descending upon our humble municipality, it would seem.'

Dwight ignored the sarcasm. 'So it would seem,' he muttered.

'Well, perhaps that is the manifestation of one of the phenomena of being a boom town. The word does get around, you know. Those who have special aptitudes and are in need of employment just naturally gravitate to such places.'

'So do a lot of other folks,' Dwight countered. 'I'd check out the fella's background pretty careful, if'n I was you.'

'Oh, come, now, Marshal!' the newsman rejoined, his eyes dancing. 'Don't be such a pessimist. Surely you believe the Almighty to be capable of sending us special blessings in times of need.'

'The Almighty can do as he pleases,' Dwight conceded, 'but I've noticed from time to time that he seems to allow some o' the devil's helpers a lot looser rein than I'd like.'

'Indeed, that seems to be true. By the same token,

40

that's what keeps newspapermen such as myself in business, so it's hard for me to complain. On the other hand, perhaps that's why he has placed you in the position of protecting us vulnerable souls from those of such ilk,' Newsome teased. 'Why, Marshal, you may very well be the instrument of the Almighty himself, sent as a protecting angel for the humble hamlet of Headland!'

Dwight chuckled in spite of himself. 'Well, now, an angel's one thing I ain't never been accused o' bein' afore.'

'Then you must consider this a banner day, Marshal.'

'Either that or a day when that there stuff on this street's some deeper'n usual.'

Newsome laughed aloud. 'Why, Marshal! Are you accusing me of unduly spreading fertilizer where no productive crops are likely to grow?'

'That is your business, ain't it?'

'Oh, come now, Marshal! How can you say such a thing? Everything in the *Headland Courier* is always and foremost of a strictly verified and factual nature.'

'Yeah, well, if you say so.'

'You will be especially interested in the lead news item in this week's edition.'

'Is that so?'

'I'm sure you will find it fascinating at the very least. It will be the first announcement the general public will have seen of the veritable rolling fortress that is about to emphasize the prosperity with which Headland has been endowed of late.'

41

Dwight frowned. 'You're puttin' a story about that new stage in your newspaper?'

'Why, of course I am, Marshal. The new Concord Armored Stagecoach that Wells Fargo has deemed us worthy of meriting in the transport of the considerable valuables from the mines and the return transport of the equally considerable payrolls of that same enterprise is news of the first magnitude.'

'You're runnin' a news item about that new stage in your newspaper?' Dwight asked again, sounding even to himself as if he were his own echo.

'Precisely. Complete with dimensions, weight, and a full description of all the security that will accompany its circuit.'

Dwight's expression as well as the sudden flush of his face made his displeasure abundantly clear. 'Now why in the Sam Hill would you go and do that?'

'Because it's news, Marshal. It's news. The *Headland Courier* is in the business of news. It is, after all, a newspaper.' He said it again, heavily emphasizing the word 'news.' '*News* paper. That's what I do.'

'But that's just invitin' every highwayman and would-be outlaw to have a crack at it! You're puttin' the lives of everyone on that stage at risk.'

'On the contrary,' Newsome argued, 'by detailing the invulnerability and the security precautions of that most remarkable conveyance, I am virtually guaranteeing that nobody will be foolish enough to make any attempt at robbery.'

'I doubt that. Publishin' all that information will just seem like an out-an'-out challenge to a lot o' guys.'

Newsome shrugged. 'Well, then, should that be the case, they can't say they were not well warned of the consequences of their ill-advised attempt to accomplish the impossible.'

'And how many guards are gonna get shot in the process?'

'That would certainly be an unfortunate eventuality,' Newsome conceded, 'but such considerations must not hamper the ethical obligation of a newspaper to publish all relevant and pertinent news.'

'That sounds like nothin' more than a highfalutin way o' sayin' you're gonna publish every bit o' gossip you can dig up.'

'Merely a matter of semantics, Marshal. What one man may consider as gossip another considers to be news. I do carefully ascertain the factual nature of what I publish. You will be interested in knowing that I personally interviewed both Hiram Birdwell, the President of the Headland Land And Mineral Bank, and Clem Adkins, the General Manager of our local branch of Wells Fargo, and I will personally attest to the factual accuracy of everything in the aforesaid news article.'

Dwight sighed with a mixture of anger and resignation. 'Ain't gonna be any good come of it, mark my words,' he warned.

He continued to scowl at the back of the newsman as Newsome walked down the street. He was not at all sure whether the knot in the middle of his stomach was anger at Walt, or a premonition of things to come. 'Maybe both,' he muttered. 'Maybe both.'

# CHAPTER 6

Ten-year-old Billy Humbolt thought his new game was just about the most fun he'd ever had. It had taken a while to get the hang of it, but once he did he honed his skill to a fare-thee-well.

It was a simple game. The blacksmith had given him the big iron hoop. It was actually a rim from a worn-out wagon wheel he'd rebanded. It was worn too thin to be used again, and the smith well knew the Humbolts could never afford toys for their ample brood of children. Delbert Andersen, or 'Dane' as he was known, had a soft spot for the boy. He showed him how to use a stick to propel the hoop forward, direct its path, and keep it upright. Once he caught on, Billy could – and constantly did – fly through town as fast as his bare feet would carry him, his hoop bouncing over rocks, sticks or road apples. He delighted in racing buggies whose drivers were game to race through town. He nearly always won those matches, because he could duck and dodge around horses and buggies much quicker than a buggy or a buckboard.

It was when he chose to use the sidewalk for his personal racetrack that he encountered problems. He thought it was great sport to slalom around pedestrians and the merchandise a few of the merchants displayed on the board sidewalk in front of their stores. Inevitably, he failed to evade someone who moved in an unexpected direction, and a collision resulted.

Still, the good-natured grin that always graced his generously freckled face and his abject apology almost always dispelled the wrath of the casualties of his youthful exuberance and lack of caution.

After each such episode he confined his hoop-racing to the street again for a time, but it was always he who was on the defensive there. Besides, the hoop and his bare feet went faster on the smoother surface of the sidewalks. The clatter of its passage over the boards only increased the feeling of speed and freedom.

It was nothing unusual, then, when Billy collided with Jarvis McCrae just as he stepped out the front door of the *Headland Courier*. Neither was it entirely an accident. Billy's constant path up and down the street infuriated Mac for some reason that nobody understood. As he stepped out the door he spotted Billy at once, approaching at his normal dead run. Instead of moving back out of the way, he stepped into the center of the sidewalk. Billy directed the hoop over to avoid him, but Mac reached out and grabbed it. With the back of his other hand he swatted the boy along the side of his head, sending the youngster sprawling into the street.

'You little heathen!' Mac shouted at him. 'Take this infernal thing and keep it off this sidewalk or so help me I'll wrap it around your head so tight you'll never get it off.'

'I'm sorry, mister,' Billy stammered, scrambling to his feet. One hand held the side of his face where Mac's hand had landed. 'I didn't mean to run into ya.'

'You are constantly running into someone,' Mac accused. 'You just lost your hoop. When you grow up enough to use some judgment, maybe I'll give it back.'

'Don't keep my hoop!' Billy protested.

'It is not your hoop any more,' Mac declared. 'It is mine now. Now begone, before I inflict a real whipping on you.'

The voice behind Mac was soft and just as carefully proper as the pressman's. It nonetheless held a distinct edge. 'I do not think that is at all called for. You had no right to hit the boy. Now give him back his hoop.'

Mac whirled to face whoever dared to interfere. Facing him was Val Lingquist, the new clerk at Glendenning's Mercantile Store. Val's expression was almost bland, but his eyes flashed with anger. Mac's own eyes bulged with elevated wrath. That someone would take the boy's side in the matter was unforgivable. That this puny, immaculately dressed little man, half his size, would dare to stand up to him was more than intolerable.

46

'Mind your own business,' he rumbled.

'I believe I just decided to make this my business,' Val replied, his tone mild, his voice even. 'When a grown man assaults a child as you just did, I believe that ought to be the business of any decent citizen.'

'I didn't do half what I should to the little whelp,' Mac fumed. 'I ought to beat him within an inch of his life.'

'You have already done far more than you had any right to do,' Val disagreed. 'Now give the boy back his hoop and be on your way.'

'What? Who are you to try to tell me what to do?'

'Well, who would you like for me to be?' Val asked with a tight smile. 'I will be happy with whatever pleases you, just so long as you do as I say.'

'It'll be a cold day in July when a sawed-off little pilgrim like you tells me anything,' Mac declared, stepping forward toward the much smaller man.

It probably wasn't the first time that Mac had badly underestimated someone. It may well have been the time he regretted the quickest. At the threat, Val moved forward instead of backing away. His right fist connected with Mac's nose with stunning force. Blood flew in all directions.

A small crowd had begun to gather as soon as Val confronted the bigger man. As the blood flew, a collective gasp escaped from almost every mouth.

Before Mac even had time to react, Val connected twice more with blows that felt like sledgehammers into Mac's mid-section. The breath went out of him with a whoosh as he bent forward.

Momentarily helpless to straighten up, Mac's face was the target of half a dozen well-placed blows in the space of two heartbeats. He staggered backward, blood already coursing down his face from cuts that the small man's iron hard fists had opened up on his eyebrows.

Even as he staggered back, one of Val's fists connected with his ribcage with a crack that indicated a fractured rib. Mac grunted, fighting to keep his balance.

The next blow seemed impossible to come from anyone Val's size. A straight right to the chin lifted the big man off his feet. He crashed backward to the sidewalk, spread-eagled and unconscious. The entire episode had taken no more than two minutes.

Ignoring both his supine antagonist and the excited buzz of the small crowd that had gathered, Val turned to Billy. His voice was still calm. He seemed not in the least out of breath. 'Are you all right, young man?'

Billy looked back and forth from Val to the unconscious form of Mac several times, as his mouth hung open. He shut his mouth, opened and shut it again, then said, 'I – I – uh, yeah. Yeah, I'm OK. Wow! I ain't never seen nobody hit anyone that hard in my life. How'd you do that? You ain't very big. I – I mean, beggin' your pardon, sir.'

Val smiled. 'You don't have to be a big man to be a good man, son. Don't ever forget that. Now you had best get your hoop and head toward home. And you might be a little more careful after this, huh?'

'Uh, yessir. I will. And . . . thanks, mister.' He headed down the street at top speed.

'That was quite a display,' a voice behind Val observed.

Val turned, moving on the balls of his feet, obviously prepared to face a new challenge. He relaxed when he recognized Dwight Stern. 'Ah. Good afternoon, Marshal,' he offered. 'I hope I am not about to be arrested for public brawling.'

Dwight shook his head. 'I saw what he did. I can't say that I ever saw anybody handle himself quite as well as that, though.'

Val shrugged, but offered no explanation. 'I did feel compelled to interfere when he decided to take the lad's hoop away from him.'

Dwight nodded. 'That's about the only thing that kid has to call his own.'

'I gathered that.'

'You're new in town. I don't think I even know your name.'

With a straight face, but with a dancing light in his eyes betraying him, Val said, 'I rather suspect that's true. You don't.'

Anger flashed in Dwight's eyes for the barest moment, then he grinned. 'Well, then, I'll ask it a different way. What's your name, Stranger?'

'No, actually it isn't.'

'Isn't what?'

'My name isn't Stranger. I have heard folks called that, but I've never really met anyone actually named that.'

49

'Keep workin' on it an' I may rethink whether I want to arrest you for public fightin',' Dwight declared, with just as straight a face. 'In fact, when that typesetter o' Newsome's wakes up, he may wanta press charges.'

'Hmm. Well, in that case, I suppose I should provide a name so you'll know who you're arresting.'

'That'd help all right.'

Val thrust a hand out to the marshal. 'Val Lindquist, at your service, Marshal.'

Dwight took the hand and returned the surprisingly strong grip. 'You're new in town.'

'That also is true. I am employed by Glendenning's Mercantile Store, as of almost a month ago.'

A curtain clouded Dwight's eyes instantly. 'Hmm. That's a bit of a coincidence. That's just about the same time that fella came to town.'

Val's eyes darted to the prone figure on the sidewalk, just beginning to stir. 'Is that so?' he responded. 'Do you happen to know where he came from?'

The sudden interest sparked an equal reaction from Dwight. 'Nope. Newsome said he just dropped in one day and asked if he needed a typesetter. Walt says he's the best help he's ever hired, settin' type an' runnin' the press both.'

'You don't say,' Val replied, his voice thoughtful. 'An experienced typesetter and pressman just happens to drift into town and seek work at the local newspaper.'

'Now why would that be of special interest to you?' Dwight demanded.

It was Val's turn to become suddenly cautious. 'No reason. I was just on my lunch hour, Marshal, so if you don't mind I'll head on down to the café and grab a bite to eat so I can get back to work. Good day.'

Without waiting for a response he turned and walked away. Dwight frowned as his practiced eye noted the bulge in the slight man's pants pocket, indicating he carried a gun that most folks would never notice. The man was certainly not what he seemed. Just one more thing to add to the list of nagging worries the marshal was beginning to fret more and more about. 'Too many things just ain't addin' up around here,' he muttered as he too walked away.

# CHAPTER 7

'This isn't news! News is somethin' that's happened. This here's an announcement. It's an invitation. This is nothin' but a formal invitation to every outlaw in the country,' Dwight yelled.

Walt Newsome held both hands up in front of him, palms toward the marshal. 'Now, now, Marshal, don't get apoplectic on me.'

Dwight waved the latest edition of the *Headland Courier* as if were a battle flag. 'Do you realize what this is gonna do? This absolutely guarantees that somebody is goin' to try to rob that stage before it ever makes its first arrival in Headland.'

'Oh, come now, Marshal,' the owner and editor of the newspaper scoffed. 'Do you really think there are hordes of outlaws and brigands lurking about the hills and valleys reading my newspaper to determine where they ought to strike next?'

'I'll tell you what,' Dwight fumed. 'Let me put an item in your newspaper that you're going to be carrying ten thousand dollars to Cheyenne, then I'll set you on a horse and head you south and see what happens to you.'

'Come, come now,' the publisher chided again, 'that is not a fair comparison and you know it. I am not an armored, fully defended, virtually impregnable mobile fortress, as this new stagecoach is. If I were, I would welcome any such attack as an opportunity to verify the futility of any and all future attacks.'

'And what if they just wait until it gets into town?' Dwight argued. 'Are you gonna guarantee someone won't get the bright idea of hittin' it when it gets unlocked to deliver those payrolls that you've advertised to the world will be on board?'

Newsome leaned back in his swivel-chair and put his feet up on his desk. 'Those payrolls being shipped in are a pittance in comparison to the amount that will be going the other direction. There will be over a month's worth of gold production from both the Gatlin Mine and the Clementine Mine, of the High Country Mining Corporation. There will be the gleanings from three privately owned mines for that same period of time. There will also be a considerable amount from both of our banks, being transported from here to Cheyenne. If someone were tempted to attempt a robbery, it will not be while the stage is approaching, but rather on its outward trip.'

'I am very well aware of all that,' Dwight retorted. 'If I hadn't already been aware of it, I would be now, since you published everything you just said and a good deal more. It wouldn't surprise me if we had the James gang, the Dalton boys and the Hole-In-The-Wall gang all combinin' forces to go after this stage. You've changed it from a well-armored stage to nothin' more than a rolling bull's-eye for every would-be crook in the country.'

'I certainly hope you're right,' Newsome responded. 'If that truly happens, just think how many unsavory and dangerous villains will be eliminated from the surrounding environs. I will make sure to mention to Mr Adkins that the guards will need an inexhaustible supply of ammunition with which to dispatch such a congregated assortment of larcenous miscreants as the country has never seen. And just think, Marshal, what a peaceable and serene territory we shall then enjoy, with all those undesirables summarily dispatched to perdition!'

Dwight opened his mouth twice to answer the jibes with which the newsman was taunting him, but each time closed his mouth. He wheeled and stomped out of the office, knowing he was about to permanently alter the printer's expression if he didn't leave. Halfway out the door he turned and raged, 'Newsome, if that stage does get attacked and any one of them guards gets killed, it'll be because of you and this dad-blamed paper. If that happens, I'll be back to arrest you for the murder of any guard that gets killed.'

He stormed out of the door, slamming it shut, then whirled around and stepped back inside. He waved the wadded paper again as he ranted, 'And for the price of any horse that gets shot!'

He slammed the door yet again behind himself and marched down the street. The wadded newspaper in his hand, the forward thrust of his head and his glowering countenance were more than adequate to forestall any greeting from passers-by as he stormed his way back to his office. He walked in and slammed the door behind him hard enough to rattle the windows. Only then did he notice Val Lindquist sitting beside the desk, regarding him curiously.

'I believe I am glad I am not the last person you talked with,' Lindquist observed. 'I'm not too sure I want to be the next one. Perhaps I'll stop back at a more opportune time.'

Dwight glared at the smaller man a long moment before his stance and expression began to soften. He took in a deep breath and let it out slowly. 'Sorry about that,' he mumbled. 'I didn't know anyone was here.'

'I rather gathered that. If I were to guess, I would say somebody has gotten under your skin rather well.'

'You could say that,' Dwight agreed, throwing the wadded up newspaper on the desk.

Val glanced at it, understanding igniting a spark in his eyes. 'Ah, yes. The newspaper. Such a formidable weapon in the right hands, and a truly frightful loose cannon in the wrong ones.'

'You read it?'

'I did. It is, in fact, the reason for my visit.'

'Oh?'

55

'I have thought at some length about our previous meeting, and I was not at all sure what impression of me that meeting left you with. I have also considered the events that appear to be transpiring, or about to do so, in this town. I felt the need to drop in and simply let you know that if and when you have a need to know, you must understand that I am firmly and solidly on your side.'

'My side of what?'

Lindquist studied him for a long moment, then said only, 'Just be aware I am on your side. That's really all I am allowed to say, at this point.'

'Do you know somethin' I don't know?'

Again the smaller man was thoughtful for a moment. Then he shook his head. 'I rather doubt it. We shall see.'

Without any further explanation he stood and walked out the door in a series of moves so smooth and graceful he almost appeared to rise and float out of the office in one continuous motion. Dwight stared after him, his brow furrowed in confusion. He mentally replayed every word the man had said, then shook his head in exasperation. 'Now how come folks can't just say what they mean?' he muttered. 'I hate it when people talk in riddles.'

# CHAPTER 8

Dwight stood and looked around his office. Ten men stood leaning against the outer walls of the small room. Behind the desk the two cells of the town's jail held only one inmate. Obviously a cowboy by his dress, the man was sprawled on the iron bunk, snoring loudly.

'Frenchy get a little frisky?' Howard Glendenning, owner of the hardware store inquired.

Dwight smiled slightly. 'Not really. Just too drunk to know what he was doin'. I figgered he'd be better off sleepin' it off in here.'

'So what's on your mind, Marshal?' Sven Carlsen interrupted. 'I take it something big is going to happen?'

Dwight sized up the men he had asked to be there. There was Frank Singler, the gunsmith; Harvey Frieden, owner of the livery barn, Soren Swenson, owner of the feed store, Isaiah Formisch, furniture maker, David Lowenberg, owner of the mercantile store, 'Dane' Andersen, the blacksmith, Virgil

Zucher, the carpenter, and Ralph Humbolt, sometimes clerk in the mercantile store, sometimes
hostler at the livery barn, sometimes anything for
which someone wanted to hire an honest and hard-
working man.

Dwight leaned back against the front of his desk.
'I'm guessin' you all read this week's paper.'

Every man there either nodded his head or
mumbled his affirmation.

'Is that what this is about?' Harvey asked.

It was Dwight's turn to nod his head. 'I've known
about it for quite a while. It's been in the works for
several months, actually. I don't know how we
managed to keep it from the professional nosy neigh-
bor this long, but he finally got wind of it. The more
I've thought about it, the more concerned I've
become. It's better than even money that somebody'll try to hit that stage before it gets here.'

A murmur of agreement came from nearly a
dozen throats.

'You wantin' a posse to ride out an' meet it?' Soren
Swenson asked.

'No,' Dwight said with a flat finality in his voice.
'Whatever happens to it outside of town isn't really
any of my business. I care, of course, but I don't have
jurisdiction anywhere but in town.'

'You think they'll hit it in town?' Harvey's voice was
incredulous.

Again Dwight nodded. 'I do. Think about it. Even
if they stopped the stage somewhere else, what are
they going to do? The guards inside are behind steel

plates. There are eight outriders. And if they managed to kill off all the guards, then what would they do? There's no way they're going to get that strongbox open. Not even with dynamite. There's no way they can carry it off. Without a block and tackle or something they couldn't even lift it off the stage. So even if someone tries to rob it on the way here, it won't do them any good.'

He paused to let what he had said soak in, then continued. 'So the reasonable thing to do would be to wait until it's unlocked at one of the banks. Then they can just take the money and run.'

'But right in town, that'd be awful risky,' Isaiah observed.

'Unless they had enough men to overpower the guards, hit fast, grab the money, and ride out. Couple that with the idea that once they're in town, the outriders and such will let their guard down.'

'Do you think somebody'd actually try that?' Harvey Frieden pondered.

'If you were an outlaw and had enough men to do it, wouldn't you?'

'How much money are we talking about?' Sven asked.

'On the way into town, over ten thousand dollars.'

'That's a lot, but not if you had to divide it up between a gang of, say, ten or fifteen men,' Howard Glendenning opined.

'That's true,' Dwight conceded. 'But what if they hit it on the way out of town, when it's loaded, before it's locked. Then we're talking about more than one hundred thousand dollars in gold and paper money put together.'

Stunned silence filled the room, saturated the air, and spilled out into the night. It weighed down on the assembled group as if it were a physical force, stifling any latent attempt to respond. It was finally Dane Andersen who dispelled the oppressive silence with, 'Are you serious?'

'Now you know why I'm scared,' Dwight assured them.

'Now I'm scared too,' Frank Singler admitted.

'So what do you want of us?' Sven asked, for the second time inside half an hour.

'I want to deputize the ten of you, have you positioned and well armed, and ready to fight a war if we have to.'

'How will we know who we are fighting against?'

'Oh, they'll make that perfectly clear,' Dwight surmised. 'They'll either cover their faces or they'll just be wavin' their guns around, or shootin' at us.'

'Shotguns would be good,' Frank said. 'Twelve- or ten-gauges. Double-ought buckshot. That way you can't miss at close range.'

'Rifles are better to just hit who you wanta hit,' Lowenberg argued. 'There'll be folks on the street.'

'For a few minutes, probably,' Dwight agreed, 'but after the first shots are fired everybody'll scramble for safety except the bad guys and us.'

Ralph's eyes reflected the trauma of too many other battlefields. 'I'd really hoped I'd seen the last of war that I'd ever see,' he bemoaned.

'So did we all,' Sven agreed, shadows of the same phantoms in his own eyes.

Virgil Zucher spoke for the first time. 'That war is over. But as long as there are evil people who prey on others there will be wars and rumors of wars, as the Good Book says. We will either stand like men and war against evil as the need arises, or we will cower from its threats and be its victims. If there are those who would attack even in the heart of town, we have no choice but to stop them.'

It was probably the longest speech any of them had ever heard from the normally laconic carpenter. None seemed willing to disturb the thoughtful silence his words evoked.

When the silence became too long, Dwight said, 'Can I count on all of you?'

A chorus of solemn and quiet responses ranged from 'Yes,' to 'Count me in,' to 'Danged right.'

'The paper said the stage was due Thursday. That's four days from now.'

Dwight nodded. 'It'll be in Thursday, along about mid-afternoon or later. We'll want to be ready by noon, then I'll have each of you get in place when we get word that it's a couple miles out. Then on Friday it'll start loadin' up about six in the mornin'. It's supposed to be loaded an' outa town by eight.'

'They're gonna load all that gold an' money in less'n two hours?'

'They're supposed to do it in less than an hour. The most dangerous time'll be when it's just about all loaded, before they get ready to lock the strongbox.'

'What do they do with the keys?' Frank wondered suddenly. 'They sure don't carry 'em along, do they?'

Dwight shook his head. 'Wells Fargo keeps 'em. The Wells Fargo office in Cheyenne has keys that match.'

'Ah! That makes sense, then.'

A dozen other questions were asked and answered. Then each man went home to decide whether to explain it all to his wife or keep it to himself.

Dwight had the same decision to make when Belinda arrived, shortly after the last man left.

She hugged Dwight briefly and kissed him lightly. 'It looked like some kind of meeting just broke up,' she observed. 'I was coming to see you, and then I noticed all the men going into your office, so I went across the street and drank coffee at Helga's until they left.'

That oppressive silence settled uncomfortably between them for a long moment. Dwight cleared his throat. 'I . . . we . . . I've been gettin' a little worried,' he fumbled.

'I saw the newspaper,' Belinda said. 'Is that what's worrying you?'

He took a deep breath. If this woman was going to be his wife, share his life, bear his children, she certainly deserved his trust. 'I'd just as soon it doesn't get noised around too much, so be sorta careful what you say. I'm worried someone's gonna try to rob that stage.'

'Are you serious? Why in the world would anyone

try to rob the most difficult to rob stage ever made?'

'Because it'll have more money than's ever been put on one stage. Ever. More'n a hundred thousand dollars.'

Belinda gasped. 'My word! Are you serious? But how would they rob it?'

'By hittin' it right here in town, before the strong-box gets locked.'

Belinda gasped. 'Really! Do you know somebody's going to do that?'

'Nope. Just a guess. And I'd guess we both know some of the ones that are in on it.'

'Are you kidding me? Who?'

He glanced at the jail cell, verifying that Frenchy was still passed out. 'How many guys that are really too smart and educated to be range bums or boom-town drifters have come into town the past three weeks or so?'

She thought about it. He could count how many she thought of, because every time she thought of another one who fit his description her head jerked up and her eyes met his.

'The printer,' she said softly, 'McCrae, because the newspaper office is where information is.'

'The carpenter, Goode, because they're working on the bank,' Dwight suggested. 'He even finagled to get me to suggest he ask for a job there.'

'That new guy who's a teller at the other bank. I don't even remember his name, but nobody seems to know where he came from.'

'What about the little guy, at the hardware store?'

Dwight said, his voice telegraphing his uncertainty.

Belinda frowned. 'I don't know. Isn't he the one that beat McCrae up for hitting the Humbolt boy?'

'Yeah, and I don't think that was something to distract me. He worked him over so fast and so good it was like something you'd go to one o' them travelin' circuses to see.'

'I heard about it.'

'There's another thing,' Dwight said, deciding to lay all his cards on the table. 'That guy – Val Lindquist he says his name is – stopped in a couple days ago. He said when I needed to know it, he wanted me to understand that he's on my side.'

'On your side? Whatever did he mean by that?'

'I don't know. That's about all he'd say. I sure have the feeling he ain't what he seems to be, though.'

'Do you really believe he's on your side?'

Dwight thought about it a long moment, then said, 'Yeah. Yeah I do. I really can't tell you why, but yeah. I do.'

He would fret about whether that was a smart decision before long.

# CHAPTER 9

He was really getting tired of this feeling. Dwight's stomach was a twisted knot that kept turning over and over. He looked up and down the street. All those people! Where did they all come from? Why couldn't they all just go home?

He knew why, and it didn't help the knot in his gut a bit. Off to the south he could already see the small dust cloud. Even as he noticed it, so did someone else. 'There she comes!' that someone else yelled.

Excitement rippled the length of Headland's main street like lightning dancing among the rocks on a mountain top. Some people started running toward the edge of town. Others crowded into the street, straining for a look at the long-expected 'Treasure Stage', as it had begun to be called.

'Bull's-Eye Stage is what it is,' Dwight muttered. 'If somebody tries to hit it when it comes into town, it's gonna be a bloodbath, with all these people in the street.'

He looked back and forth, up and down the street.

He glanced up at the four second floor balconies that Main Street boasted. His ad hoc posse was all in place. They were poised in positions where they had the best chance he could give them, should a robbery attempt take place. One member of that group was also placed inside each of the banks that was receiving a shipment of cash for the various payrolls that were being delivered. The others were placed strategically along the street. In addition, each bank had hired a couple extra guards. It seemed to be about all anyone could do.

'I'm presuming those are your men on the balconies?' a quiet voice at Dwight's shoulder asked.

Dwight jumped, his hand streaking to his gun. He hadn't heard Val Lindquist walk up beside him. 'Sorry,' the smaller man said. 'I didn't mean to startle you.'

'I guess I'm kinda jumpy.'

'I would guess you have reason to be.'

'Who are you?' Dwight asked abruptly.

Val grinned. 'Just who I said. Val Lindquist, at your service. Yours and Pinkerton's, that is.'

'Pinkerton! The detective outfit?'

'One and the same.'

'What's Pinkerton got to do with this?'

'The company is under contract to ensure the safety of this new stagecoach's deliveries. Half of the outriders who will be accompanying it are also in the employ of the agency.'

'You don't say! Is that what you meant when you said you're on my side?'

'Precisely. I was under orders not to disclose my connection until the day of the stagecoach's arrival, in order to be better able to assess who might be plotting something. I grew worried that I wouldn't have time to let you know if something happened too quickly, so I took the precaution of trying to keep you from shooting me if the festivities were initiated too quickly.'

'Are you as good with that hideout gun you carry as you are with your fists?'

Val grinned. 'I guessed you would have noticed it. Yes. Better, actually.'

Dwight fished in his pocket and pulled out a misshapen glob of lead. 'This wouldn't happen to belong to it, would it?'

'Ah! You retrieved my bullet. I'm afraid it's no longer useable.'

'How'd you end up in that deal?'

'I chanced to see the man watching you when you were dealing with a rather inebriated cowboy. I saw him walk into that space between stores. Unfortunately I didn't realize what he was up to before he shot at you. You were most fortunate. You walked right behind that post just as he fired, I believe. I returned his fire at almost the same time you did. Quite obviously, we both missed.'

Dwight studied the approaching stage. 'So you're backin' me up on this deal?'

'I am, to be sure. I also have another small ace in the hole, that I was just about to go get.'

'What's that?'

'Have you seen one of Colt's new revolving shotguns?'

'Revolving shotgun? Never heard o' such a thing.'

'Not too many folks have. It is a twelve gauge shotgun, with six barrels. It operates exactly like a sixshooter, except that the cylinder extends all the way to the end, so it has six barrels. It will fire six shotgun shells as rapidly as you can squeeze the trigger. It has pretty short barrels, so the shot spreads quite rapidly. It is truly a fearsome weapon at close range.'

'And you've got one o' them.'

'That I do. It and I will be idling at the corner of the Land and Mineral Bank. If nothing happens there, I will amble along to the Wells Fargo along with the stage.'

'They ain't likely to hit it today,' Dwight said, almost to himself.

'I suspect you're right,' Val agreed. 'There are too many people in the way. I doubt the ones involved care how many of them might get killed, but a general panic would certainly interfere with any kind of rapid getaway.'

'You know who's plannin' somethin'?'

'In a way.'

'What do you mean, "In a way"? Do you or don't you?'

Val took a deep breath, clearly deciding what or how much to share with the marshal. 'We have had information for some time that a man by the name of Will Bandy has been recruiting men for a major robbery. He has helped Johnny Rivers to escape from

68

prison in Kansas. Our information says they have been joined by a man named Jesse Wrigley. How many more they have recruited is anybody's guess.'

'Do you know any of them by sight?'

'Only Rivers. I am the one who arrested him.'

'How many of these drifters who've come into town are part of it?'

'Three that I would guess are part of it. It's pure guess, though.'

'McCrae, Goode, and Tighson?'

'Very good, Marshal! You have made the same guesses I have.'

'Here it comes.'

It might just as well have been a traveling circus, the president, and a rajah riding an elephant, all arriving simultaneously. If there were a single citizen of Headland who wasn't in the street, it was because he was either sick or in jail. Men were waving their hats in the air. The second floor windows of buildings that had a second story were jammed with faces peering downward. Children of all ages were running at top speed toward the approaching stagecoach. Soon the shouting, cheering mob completely surrounded the strange-looking Concord.

If the eight-horse team hadn't been worn down to the point of exhaustion they would certainly have bolted. Even fatigued as they were, their eyes rolled and their ears lay back flat against their heads. Fighting against the bits and tossing their heads, they lost the power of teamwork. They struggled more and more to keep the inordinately heavy vehicle moving forward.

Two of the horses caught Dwight's immediate attention. One was the biggest Belgian he had ever seen, hitched as the inside lead horse. Even more striking was an even larger Lithuanian Draft horse, hitched in the outside wheel position. It was only the steady aplomb of those two that prevented the total panic of the rest of the team. The two of them, each weighing well over 1,800 pounds, blandly ignored the tumult surrounding them and kept their attention riveted on the road ahead. Their calm demeanor and the fatigue of the whole team won the day. Little by little the driver was able to steady the rest of the team, and keep it headed toward the Wells Fargo Bank.

The outriders fought their way through the crowd, trying to keep next to the stagecoach without trampling anyone. At the bank they leaped from their horses and used their rifles as iron bars, to push against the crowd, forcing them back away, clearing a path between the stagecoach and the bank.

One less than sober fellow pushed his way to the opposite side of the stage and stuck his face up to the cross shaped slots in the iron side of the coach. No sooner had he done so than a rifle butt smashed against his face from inside the coach, breaking his nose and sending him sprawling into the street.

Nobody offered to help him up. Some stood in open-mouthed amazement. All took a step or two back away, finally giving the team and coach a circle of cleared space.

Four of the outriders climbed to the top of the stage. As if it were scripted and rehearsed, each took a position at a corner of the coach's roof, knelt on one knee, rifle held at the ready, scanning the crowd and the surrounding buildings.

A hush slowly settled across the crowd. Clem Adkins, general manager of the Headland branch of Wells Fargo stage line, pushed his way through the crowd. 'Make way! Make way!' he kept shouting as he shoved people out of his way.

When he emerged into the cleared circle he stopped, looked around with an overt air of self-importance. He pulled a ring with a single key from his vest pocket, marched to the stage, and climbed up to the top. One at a time he unlocked and removed the large padlocks from the strongbox. He stood at the end of it, farthest from the side toward the bank.

As he did, four men emerged from their positions just inside the bank door and climbed up on to the stage. Two of them lifted and held the heavy hinged lid of the strongbox.

'This is it,' Dwight muttered. 'If they're gonna hit, it's gonna be right quick now.'

His eyes darted here and there, looking for the telltale signs of approaching trouble. Some part of his mind was aware of Val Lindquist, mirroring his actions and his look of ready apprehension.

One by one, Dwight made eye contact with each of the ten men he had carefully positioned. None gave any indication of alarm.

Bags of money were handed down from the top of the stage to men on the ground. They carried them quickly into the Wells Fargo Bank. The door of the bank slammed shut behind them.

The two men holding the lid of the strongbox lowered it back down, but Adkins eschewed locking the padlocks again. Instead he seated himself on the box and nodded to the driver.

The driver yelled, 'Heeyaah!' and snapped the reins against the backs of the team. Reluctantly they leaned into their harnesses. Slowly the heavy coach began to move again. With the circle of entranced citizens surrounding it, it lumbered a little more than a block down the street and stopped in front of the Headland Land & Mineral Bank.

Obviously watching for it, two men emerged instantly from that bank. Bags of money were handed down to them as well. The scene just enacted at the Wells Fargo Bank was repeated. When the money was safely ensconced in that bank's vault, Dwight felt a huge relief rush through him.

'That's all folks!' Clem Adkins announced from his perch atop the stage. 'Show's over.'

He climbed down, followed by the guards, who were noticeably more relaxed. The men began to joke and jostle one another, as they headed across the street for one or another of the saloons, or to where duty had been left suspended by the stage's arrival. The driver and shotgun guard were left on their own to move the stage to its quarters and take care of the team.

'Well, we got by that one,' Val said softly at Dwight's shoulder.

Dwight nodded. 'At least there oughta be a whole lot less people in the way in the mornin'.'

'Let's hope so,' Val observed.

The relief Dwight had felt at the successful offloading hadn't lasted long. The tight knot was back in his stomach. He knew the big test was still to come. He wouldn't sleep much tonight. He had no way to know how much he would need the sleep, before his job was finished.

# CHAPTER 10

Death and destruction send no publicity notices in advance of their coming.

Soft early morning sunlight bathed Headland's Main Street in a deceptive cloak of serenity. In the trees that had survived the town's building boom, birds blithely chirped their welcome to the new day. In the prairie grasses surrounding the town meadow larks added the blind optimism of their lilting melodies. Even the absence of any breeze seemed to contribute a sense of peace and well-being.

The pretense of peacefulness was not echoed in Marshal Dwight Stern's visage. Shadows around his eyes gave witness to the near-sleepless night he had spent. The breakfast of pancakes, sidepork, eggs and coffee had done nothing to relieve the knot in his belly. His eyes darted here and there, leaping to any new movement they detected, poking into the shadows between buildings, then lifting to scan the distant reaches of the roads leading into town. Not even a small hint of stirred dust indicated the approach of any danger.

Val Lindquist appeared abruptly and silently beside him. 'All quiet so far,' he said.

'So far,' Dwight agreed.

'Everyone in place?'

'They're all there.'

'At least it does not resemble a circus this morning.'

'I'm surprised half the town didn't beat the sun up this mornin', just to get in the way.'

'I am not complaining.'

'Here it comes.'

Both men turned their heads to watch the approach of the armored stagecoach that had entered town only the night before. A fresh team of eight horses seemed to pull it with ease, in spite of the weight of its iron sides and top. The reinforced strongbox securely welded to the iron plate that covered the top added considerably to that weight. Even so, the vehicle rolled with what appeared to be surprising ease. 'They must have awful good races in them wheels,' Dwight observed.

'A great deal of axle grease, too, I'm sure. It would be my guess they will wear out rather quickly, nonetheless.'

The conveyance halted amidst a cloud of dust in front of the Headland Land & Mineral Bank. Immediately Clem Adkins, general manager of the Wells Fargo stage line climbed to the top and removed the padlocks from the strongbox. He had no sooner done so than several men began a bucket brigade style line, passing gold bars from hand to hand, then up to the top of the stagecoach. There they were stacked into the strongbox.

Dwight smiled as he watched the course of the first gold bar. Every man who took it nearly dropped it, surprised at the weight of such a small ingot of metal. After that first one, they were all much better prepared for the weight, and passed each along easily.

After the gold was loaded, three bags of money were passed along the same way, all under the watchful eyes of Hiram Birdwell, president of the bank.

'I don't understand why they ship bags of paper money in, then turn right around and ship bags of paper money back out again.' Dwight muttered.

'Don't try to understand the ways banks work,' Val advised. 'You'll only get more confused.'

'That's it!' Birdwell proclaimed when the last of the money was in the strongbox.

As if that were the signal, the stage driver yelled, 'Heeyah, fellas. Hie on there!' as he slapped the backs of the horses with the reins.

The horses leaned into their harnesses as Dwight scanned the doors and windows of the empty street. All was quiet. It was far too quiet. It was going far too well.

'Something is coming,' Val said softly.

Dwight's eyes jerked up to follow the direction of the smaller man's pointing finger. A small dust cloud was approaching from the south. 'Wagon,' Dwight said.

'Looks like it.'

'Four riders as well.'

'Looks like it.'

'It wouldn't likely be a rancher, with four riders staying with the wagon.'

'Nope.'

'I'll make sure the men at the other bank are ready, just in case.'

Dwight began to gesture to his men, alerting them to the approach of some unidentified arrivals.

It might have been the warning that gave two men the opportunity they needed. On each of two of the balconies, a man stepped out and summarily shot the man Dwight had stationed there.

The two shots were so closely spaced that Dwight wasn't sure whether it was two, or whether it was one shot and an echo. His gun was in his hand instantly. As if it had a mind of its own, it lifted to the balcony from where he had seen, from the corner of his eye, his man topple. He fired at the gunman an instant before the gunman's second shot hurtled toward him. That split second caused the gunman's shot to go wide. The bullet from Dwight's gun shattered his heart and drove him backward into the room from which he had just emerged.

Lost in the roar of those shots was the slightly lighter report of Val Lindquist's forty-one-caliber Colt. He just as quickly sent two bullets into the heart of the man who had murdered the guard on the second balcony.

On a third balcony, Frank Singler had spotted a gun as it emerged from a second story window across the street, just before it spouted fire and lead in his direction. He flopped to the floor and with some part of his mind noted the glass shattering where he had been an instant before. He fired three rounds into that window in extremely rapid fire. He was rewarded by a yell of pain, and the disappearance of the gun barrel.

The other members of the ad hoc posse ducked for cover, guns at the ready, scanning around for any others bent on robbery.

The approaching wagon was already at the end of Main Street, the driver urging the horses to top speed. The extra man on the driver's seat aimed a rifle toward one of the posse members. Half a dozen bullets instantly riddled his body.

Two men carrying bags of money from the Wells Fargo Bank stopped in mid-stride, gaping at the sudden burst of activity, clearly undecided whether to hurry to the stage or duck back inside the bank.

Clem Adkins grabbed the lid of the strongbox, jerking it from the hands of the two men holding it, slamming it shut with a resounding clang. He grabbed one of the padlocks, fumbling frantically to get it into the loop of one of the heavy hasps. He grunted, dropped the padlock, took a step backward and toppled from the top of the stage, into the street.

Dwight took aim at the rider beside the approaching wagon who had shot Adkins. Before he could fire a sharp voice behind him hollered, 'Hold it right there! Everybody hold your fire, or the woman gets her head blown off.'

Dwight whirled. His heart instantly dropped to someplace in the bottom of his stomach. Val Lindquist, who had whirled in the same instant, swore softly.

Jarvis McCrae gripped the back of Belinda Holdridge's dress with one hand. In the other hand he held a short double-barreled shotgun.

Dwight assessed the situation and swiftly lowered his gun. 'Hold your fire!' he ordered at the top of his voice.

'You'd better all hold your fire!' McCrae yelled, triumph unmistakable in his voice. 'I've got the triggers of this shotgun wired back. My thumb is all that's holding the hammers back. Both barrels are against this woman's head. If anything causes me to relax my grip, or slip in any way, both barrels will go off, and it will blow her head clear off her shoulders.'

A dozen pair of bulging eyes quickly ascertained that he was telling the truth. Mouths gaped. Guns lowered. All eyes turned to Dwight.

Clearly torn between his duty and his love, Dwight already knew he was incapable of causing the death of his beloved. Even if it had been a stranger he would have had no less choice. He could not willingly sacrifice a life to save a pile of gold.

Belinda's eyes looked at Dwight imploringly. 'I . . . I'm sorry, sweetheart! I didn't even hear him come into the house. The first thing I knew was the gun against the back of my head.'

Dwight holstered his gun, but kept his hand near it. He prayed that in the minutes to come Mac would grow careless enough to move the gun away from the back of Belinda's head momentarily. All he needed was a split second.

He made no plea to the gunman. He knew anything he could say would fall on deaf ears.

'That's Rivers, on the right side of the wagon,' Val spoke softly beside him.

'Likely Bandy drivin' the wagon.'

'That would be my guess. He fits the description.'

McCrae ignored them. 'You boys on top o' the stage, lay your guns down and climb down.'

They did so, glaring helplessly at McCrae. When they were off the stage and lined up along the front of the bank, he yelled, 'Now you – the driver. Get that brake set and wrap the lines around it.'

The driver complied.

'Now you and the shotgun guard drop your guns off the side and climb down.'

They complied wordlessly.

The wagon passed the stage, wheeled in a wide circle, drove up almost against the side of the stage-coach and halted. Instantly half a dozen men, including Les Goode and Walt Tighson, climbed into the wagon, then up on to the stagecoach. They swiftly removed the gold bars and money bags from the open strongbox and transferred it all to the waiting wagon.

'That's all of it,' one of them announced to the man on the wagon's driver's seat.

From the wagon, Bandy called to McCrae. 'Bring the woman.'

Instead of speaking, Mac jabbed Belinda in the back of the head with the shotgun barrels. She started to whirl toward him in anger, but he shoved her forward, jabbing her again with the gun barrels. Her eyes blazed, but she complied.

She considered defying him, daring him to shoot her, but she was certain he would do so without hesitation. She briefly considered just relaxing and falling straight downward. She knew Dwight only needed one brief instant of opportunity. The tight grip Mac maintained in the twist of her dress, right between her shoulders, convinced her that she couldn't accomplish that either.

At the back of the wagon she hesitated. Dwight had carefully edged closer as the treasure was being transferred. He was less than twenty feet from the back of the wagon. Belinda looked into his eyes, her own pleading silently.

Dwight was watching Mac instead of Belinda. He was certain there would be an instant during her climb into the wagon that those deadly gun barrels would stray from the back of her head.

He was wrong. With an uncanny ability, Mac kept the cold and deadly steel within an inch of her head as she clambered up and into the back of the wagon. With amazing agility, he followed her into the wagon, the gun never wavering from its deadly focus.

It was Mac who spoke then. 'If anybody follows us, or anybody takes a pot-shot at one of us while we are leaving, she gets her head blown off.'

Bandy slapped the reins and clucked to the

81

wagon's team. They leaned into their harnesses and the wagon quickly moved down the road, a small cloud of dust marking its progress.

Dwight watched it draw ever farther away, a feeling of helpless rage making the previous knot in his stomach seem trifling by comparison. He knew, with an utter certainty that he fought with all his will, that he would never hold the woman he loved in his arms again. He knew just as certainly that he would find a way to rescue her, or avenge her, or die trying.

# CHAPTER 11

Helpless rage held Dwight in its thrall for several minutes. The dust cloud left by the fleeing wagon settled slowly on to the sage and bunchgrass. Half a dozen ideas fluttered through the marshal's mind, each being discarded as quickly as it arose.

Val stepped up beside him. 'Harvey's gettin' our horses. You want a posse gotten together?'

Dwight shook his head. 'No. Well, yeah, but I don't want 'em leavin' yet. They'll be watchin' their backtrail. Just as soon as a posse puts up a dust cloud, they'll kill Belinda.'

'So what's the plan?'

'I've been standin' here tryin' to figure out where they'll stop. They ain't likely goin' far with that wagon. Too slow. Too heavy. Too easy to follow. They'll be stoppin' to divide up the gold pretty soon. If we can figure out where they're gonna do that, we might be able to slip up on 'em.'

'Got any ideas?'

'A couple. It looked like they turned off the road

a little more than a mile south. Turned east, it looked like, from what dust they was stirrin' up.'

'Is there a place in that area that would serve their purpose well?'

'A couple at least. The problem is, they're both where a couple lookouts would see anyone comin' from half a mile away.'

'That could present a problem.'

'We almost have to figure out how to get at 'em from the far side.'

'And do it before they have opportunity to divide up the loot and split up.'

'Ain't no way we're gonna do that. They'll have that done afore we're half way there.'

'Are you adept at tracking?'

'Yup.'

'Two of our men are dead.'

'Isaiah an' Howard?'

'Yes.'

'How many o' them?'

'Four.'

'That leaves eight, by my count.'

'Four we know, and four we do not.'

'I'll know 'em all when I see 'em.'

Harvey arrived just then with their horses. Val's saddle held two long-gun scabbards. Into one he slid his thirty-thirty. The other was shorter and wider. The Colt revolving shotgun slid into it as if it were made for it.

'You want the rest of us to tail ya?' Harvey asked.

'Yeah. Mount as many men as you can in a hurry.

Wait an hour. Ten to one they'll split up. Try to have at least two men to follow each one. If you can, have at least one man that's a decent tracker in each pair. Lindquist and I'll try to catch up to 'em afore they get split up, but that ain't likely.'

Hiram Birdwell arrived somewhat out of breath. 'Marshal, it is imperative you overtake those brigands and recover my gold. My bank cannot afford to suffer such a loss. I have lost only one of my guards, but I have lost all that gold! And a good deal of money besides! It was all entrusted to me. Your duty demands that you recover it, Marshal!'

Instead of answering, Dwight swung into the saddle. He slid his forty-four-forty into its scabbard as he nudged his horse forward. At the edge of town he turned at right angles away from the road. A hundred yards from the road he descended into a shallow arroyo. He turned and followed the bottom of it in the general direction the robbers had fled.

He and Val rode at a swift trot, resisting the urge to run their horses. They knew instinctively they were embarking on a long chase, and stamina would be more important in the long run than speed.

'That bunch will raise quite a dust when they manage to ride out of town,' Val observed when a wide spot in the gully allowed them to ride abreast.

'I'm countin' on that,' Dwight replied. 'If they're watchin' the dust cloud comin' from them, they're less likely to be watchin' the direction we're comin' from.'

'How far are these places where you presume they

85

will stop and divide their plunder?'

'Not more'n about four miles. They're likely already there, in fact.'

As they rode, Dwight watched for spots where the dry gulch's rim was so low that he could almost see over it. At one such spot he stopped his horse, grasped the saddle horn, placed one knee behind the cantle, then placed the other foot in the saddle. He moved the other foot beside it, removed his hat, then stood, balancing on the saddle, peering over the rim of the gully.

The horse stood rock still, allowing him to remain balanced. 'That's odd,' he muttered.

'What?' Val replied instantly.

'Someone's comin' this way. On foot.'

'On foot?'

'Runnin'.'

He spread his feet apart, allowing him to drop into the saddle, and dismounted swiftly. Val did likewise, and the two climbed the side of the gully. Dwight again removed his hat, but Val decided not to remove his smaller bowler, which he always wore. Both men peered carefully over the gully's rim.

'It's a kid,' Dwight said.

'I do believe it is the Humbolt lad,' Val offered.

'What's he doin' out here?'

'You don't suppose he followed them, do you?'

Dwight didn't answer. He waited until the fleet-footed boy was nearly abreast of them, then called out to him softly. 'Billy!'

The boy jerked his head toward the voice, tangled

his foot in a clump of sage brush, and fell headlong in a tangle of arms and legs. He scrambled to his feet, eyes wide, head swiveling back and forth, seeking the source of the voice.

'Over here,' Dwight said.

'Who's there?' the boy demanded.

'Marshal Stern.'

The boy instantly turned and ran toward them. 'Boy, Marshal! Am I ever glad to see you! Oh, hello, Mr Lindquist. You too.'

'What're you doin' out here? What're you runnin' from?' Dwight demanded.

'Ain't runnin' from nothin'. Runnin' after you. I done follered 'em.'

'Followed who?'

'Them guys what stole all the gold.'

'You followed the wagon?'

'Yeah. I stayed way off to the side, like you guys is doin', so's they wouldn't see me. That wagon's heavy, so they wasn't goin' very fast. 'Sides, they was sure you wasn't gonna chase 'em, since they got your woman.'

'Did you see where they went?'

'Yeah. Well, kinda. That's what I was hustlin' back to town to tell ya. They turned off the road there at that big ol' wide gully that goes east, just afore the road starts up the big hill.'

'That makes sense,' Dwight agreed. 'They wouldn't want to make the long pull up Hartwell Hill if they didn't have to.'

'The wagon wouldn't be nearly as heavy as the stagecoach,' Val observed. 'It's all the steel that armors the stage that makes it so heavy.'

'Yeah, but that much gold's plenty heavy all by itself,' Dwight disagreed. 'Besides, they only had a two-horse team, and they ain't near as big as the ones pullin' the stage.'

'Morgans,' Val said.

Dwight simply nodded, confirming that he, too, had made note of that fact. He spoke to the boy. 'Billy, you go ahead to town. You don't need to run, and you can stay on the road. You should meet the posse before you get to town. Tell them what you told us, and tell them we're going to circle around to the east and try to catch up to the robbers before they split up, but we aren't likely to. Tell them we'll mark the trail of the ones we're following, so they can split into pairs and follow the others.'

'You're gonna get 'em chased down afore they do somethin' to Miss Holdridge, ain't ya, Marshal?'

'I'm sure gonna try,' Dwight assured him.

Even as he said it, he knew his chances of success were pretty slim.

# CHAPTER 12

'We are sufficiently far from those you are so terrified of. You can get that thing away from the back of my head now!'

Mac thought of several things to say, but held his tongue. His arm was growing awfully tired of holding both Belinda and the shotgun anyway. He swung the shotgun away from her and pointed it over the side of the wagon. He lowered the hammers, then flexed his hand several times, restoring the circulation to his fingers.

Belinda turned toward him, her face a mixture of rage and fear. 'You know that Dwight will track you down and kill you,' she declared.

'He'll try. No doubt about that,' Mac agreed. 'Whether he will succeed remains to be seen. Other people have tried. They're all dead.'

Instead of waiting for an answer from her, he turned to the driver. 'You got my horse waitin' for us, Will?'

Without turning around, Bandy said, 'The horses are waiting. Yours, mine and the ones for the boys that were in town. Three extras, since I think three of our men were killed in town.'

'Four,' Mac corrected. 'If you hadn't gotten in such an all-fired hurry, we wouldn't have needed to lose any. You knew I was gonna grab the girl.'

'I knew you were going to try,' Bandy corrected. 'There's many a slip 'twixt the cup and the lip.'

'Yeah, well, I don't slip. When I tell you I'll do something, I do it.'

'No matter,' Bandy soothed. 'Just four less to divide all this gold amongst.'

'That much more to weigh us down and slow us up,' Mac argued. 'That stuff's heavy.'

'Ah, the burden of great wealth.' Bandy almost mocked the other's concern.

'I don't see anybody following us yet. I don't like that.'

'They will be afraid to follow, so long as we have the woman. Once we get rid of her, it will be a different story.'

'What makes you think I plan to get rid of her?'

'You surely aren't thinking of taking her with you, are you?'

'Why not? She's a real looker. Feisty, too. I plan to get enough fun out of her to make up for the time I spent with my hands back in printer's ink. Not to mention the whipping I took from that pint-sized dude. I wonder who he is, anyway?'

'Johnny recognized him. He is a Pinkerton detective by the name of Val Lindquist. He is the one that arrested Johnny.'

'Then why didn't he shoot him while he had the chance?'

'He would have, if you hadn't chosen that moment to grab the woman. If any of us had started shooting after that, they would have decided they were all going to be shot, and had nothing to lose. Then they would have opened up on us regardless of the hostage.'

'So he passed up on the chance to get even with the guy that arrested him!'

'He believes he will get another chance. You can bet your bottom dollar that he, at least, will try to follow us.'

'It's a good thing we had this deal with the woman figured out ahead of time. They were really set up for us! How'd they know we were coming?'

Bandy merely shrugged. He turned the team off the road just at the bottom of a long hill. He steered them into the bottom of a broad, shallow draw that led off to the east.

Leaving the road slowed their progress considerably. The horses were forced to wend their way around clumps of brush, soap weeds and rocks. The grass and uneven ground lent more resistance to the wheels. The group of outlaws on horseback drew steadily farther ahead of them.

Feigning resignation, Belinda watched desperately for a spot where she might lunge over the side of the wagon and duck behind cover before her captor could

91

react. As she did, she listened to their conversation.

'I guess it doesn't matter,' Mac said finally. 'We got what we came for. Not to mention this rather delightful little bundle of pleasure to boot.'

As he said it he reached out a hand, lifted her chin and leered at her. The look in his eyes sent shivers through her, try as she might to hide the fact.

Bandy's disapproval was obvious, even though his back was turned. 'You had best give up the idea of taking her with you,' he advised. 'That can only lead to more problems than you can handle. When we get where we will divide the fruits of our labors, let her start walking back toward town.'

'Not a chance,' Mac said flatly. 'I been on good behavior way too long. I'm not about to miss out on having my fun with her.'

'Taking advantage of her will almost guarantee that your misdeeds will catch up with you. Some things the Good Lord may wink at. Wanton abuse of a virtuous woman is not among them.'

Mac laughed. 'Well, now, aren't you sounding just like a preacher! Where did you learn to be so high and holy?'

'I am, in point of fact, an ordained minister of the Gospel,' Bandy retorted.

Belinda's jaw dropped. Mac stared at the outlaw leader's back for a long moment in silence, before he said, 'What? Are you serious?'

'I am most serious.'

'Then what are you doing setting up the biggest hold-up Wyoming Territory has ever seen?'

They rode in silence a long way. Mac waited as long as his curiosity could stand, then pressed for an explanation. 'So what changed you from a preacher to a bank robber?'

Again a long silence ensued. At last Bandy said, 'I suppose the idea developed slowly, once I realized that the leaders of virtually every congregation perceive it as their divine duty to starve every member of the clergy as nearly as possible to death, all in the name of stewardship. They universally seek to squeeze the last dregs of service they possibly can from their ministers, while compensating them just as little as humanly possible. They bristle at and revile any and every perceived fault or misstatement. They provide only the most shabby and drafty places to live, often furnished with cast-offs which are no longer fit for their own families to use. At some point I began to resent their obvious, even ostentatious prosperity and my own poverty. When my wife died of pneumonia one cold winter, I determined to tolerate no more of their pious larceny. I gave the lot of them the tongue-lashing of their lives at prayer meeting one midweek evening. Then I emptied the pockets of the penurious penitents at gunpoint, and made my well-planned escape.'

Mac laughed uproariously. 'I would have given half my haul on this job just to've seen that!'

Sensing her opportunity, Belinda grasped the side of the wagon, swung her feet over the side and shoved herself as far from it as she could. The rear wheel just brushed her hand as she catapulted away from it. She landed on an uneven spot of ground, twisted her ankle and fell awkwardly. She scrambled to her feet, ducked behind a large boulder and began to run as fast as she could, directly away from the wagon.

It was not a good decision. Away from the wagon, to the side, meant toward the side of the gully. Shallow though it was, climbing up its side slowed her flight. So also did the stabbing pain in her ankle. She had made it no more than a dozen yards from the wagon when a cursing McCrae grasped her by the hair and jerked her backward. She sprawled painfully on the ground, the breath driven from her lungs.

Mac kept his grip on her hair and hauled her to her feet. His face inches from hers, he continued to curse, telling her in the most graphic of terms the things he was going to do to her before he let her crawl back to her precious marshal, if she managed to live long enough to do so.

He dragged her back to the wagon, still holding her by the hair. He grabbed the back of her dress and, using it and her hair, heaved her back into the wagon. She landed on the stack of gold bars in the center of the wagon. Another wave of pain shot through her from the small of her back where it contacted the edge of that stack of gold. She raised her head only to have Mac knock her flat again with the back of his hand on the side of her face.

She laid there, fighting to breathe, trying desperately not to cry nor scream.

Bandy urged the team back into motion as one of the other outlaws appeared in front of them. 'You guys are takin' your sweet time,' he challenged. 'Kick them horses up a notch.'

'I have no desire to break a wheel on a rock and disrupt our well-laid plans,' Bandy responded in a carefully measured voice. 'Do you have lookouts posted?'

'Yeah, we got a guy on top of a knoll, a-watchin'. Ain't nobody even started out yet, don't look like.'

In minutes the wagon pulled into a broad, smooth space where the gully widened out. Several horses waited patiently. Five men stood waiting less patiently than their horses. The sixth man remained on his mount. Bandy reined the team to a halt and wrapped the lines around the brake.

'Johnny and Nels, start counting the money in the bags, and divide it into eight stacks. Jesse and Arthur, count the bars of gold. The rest of you get everybody's saddle-bags over here so we can do this quickly.'

'What if it won't all fit.'

'Now there is a problem the Lord's servants are inexperienced to deal with,' Bandy chuckled. He was hurriedly replacing the clothes he had been wearing with a broadcloth suit, seemingly oblivious to Belinda's presence. 'If there is more wealth than we can carry, we shall simply have to leave the remainder here. Remember, the more gold you carry away with you, the slower your flight will be, and pursuit will be sure to come.'

It took surprisingly little time for them to count and divide the neatly bundled packets of paper money. It appeared that it, alone, would nearly fill the waiting saddle-bags.

'Put what gold you wish to carry in your saddle-bags first. You may wish to leave behind the usual contents of those bags, knowing you can readily replace it all with the money in hand. Then place a few gold bars in your bedrolls, but be sure they are folded in place securely. They are extremely heavy, and will work their way out if they are not. It would be ironic indeed if our pursuers were to capture you following a trail of golden ingots instead of bread-crumbs!'

He laughed as if he had just told the world's funniest joke. Nobody else laughed. They were all too busy counting, dividing, or grabbing their share of the fruits of their robbery.

Amazingly, they were able to distribute the several hundred pounds of gold and all the paper money, secure it and ride away.

As the first of the group started to leave, Bandy offered, 'Do not push your horses too hard, or they will tire too quickly. They are carrying the equivalent of an extra rider.'

Nobody paid the least attention to him. He mounted his own horse and, leading the horse of one of the dead outlaws, he left at a trot, continuing eastward along the bottom of the draw the wagon had followed.

Belinda's mind was churning furiously. She well

knew that flight was impossible. She had no gun, and certainly could not overpower her captor. Her eyes fell on the lace that decorated the front of her dress. Three rows of the lace were spaced horizontally across the skirt of the garment. Pretending resignation, she sat down on a large boulder, her back mostly toward those of the outlaws who had not yet left. Working as rapidly and silently as possible, she tore half a dozen pieces of lace from the dress's decor. She wadded them up and stuffed them into her pocket.

Mac had divided his share of the loot on to two horses. He motioned toward one of the animals. 'Get on.'

She hesitated the barest moment, then rose from the boulder and complied. 'Just so you know,' Mac told her, 'if you try anything funny like tryin' to run off on me, I'll strip you naked and make you ride that way in the sun. It won't take an hour afore you're plumb fried, and you'll find out what real pain is. In two hours you'll have blisters the size of your thumb all over you and you'll be screaming like a baby with the pain. And it won't keep me from having the full measure of fun I have planned with you when we get where we're going, but you'll be in so much pain by then you won't even care.'

She gasped at his words, her face paling to a sickly, ashen hue. She swallowed hard, after three attempts. She did not for an instant doubt the man's ability to be every bit as cruel as he threatened.

It took every ounce of courage she could muster to

97

slip a piece of the lace out of her pocket and drop it beside her horse as they rode away.

# CHAPTER 13

'There's eight of 'em. Two to one they're goin' eight different directions outa here.'

Without looking at Dwight, Val replied, 'I'm sure you're right.'

Wordlessly, as though they had ridden together for years, both men dismounted. Working in opposite directions, they began walking a large circle around the flat bottom of the vale, where the horseless wagon, bereft of its treasure, stood forlorn and deserted.

Odds and ends of everything imaginable were strewn about the area. Several neckerchiefs, tins of Arbuckle, hardtack, boot repair kits, even several guns and boxes of ammunition had been cast aside as the outlaws made all available space in their saddle-bags.

'I'd bet half of 'em even stuffed their shirts full o' paper money,' Dwight mused.

Every little way he spotted where a lone rider had fled, all heading east or south, away from the road that led out from town. 'Expectin' someone to be chasin' 'em pretty soon,' he mused.

He and Val met almost exactly halfway around the circle. 'I counted six horses headin' out this way,' Dwight offered.

'Five that way,' Val responded.

'McCrae rode in the wagon,' Dwight mused. 'Goode and Tighson had horses saddled and ready, and they rode 'em out. One o' the gang was shot off'n his horse, an' they took that horse with 'em.'

'McCrae had obviously planned on bringing the hostage with the wagon, so his horse would most likely have been left here, along with Bandy's,' Val added, following Dwight's line of reasoning.

'So countin' the team, they had eleven horses, but only nine people, includin' Belinda.'

'I cut two trails with two horses together.'

'I spotted one.'

'So two of them have an extra horse, each carrying only half as much money. The other one has Belinda.'

'MacRae.'

'Which is the one you'll be following, I'm sure.'

'Providin' I can figure out which one it is,' Dwight responded. The terror he kept carefully tethered in his mind nonetheless echoed in his voice.

Silence descended between the two for a long moment. It was Val who offered, then, 'Let's follow the double sets for a little ways. Maybe we can figure out which extra horses are carrying money and which one is carrying her.'

The suggestion rang hollow in Dwight's mind. Her weight on a horse would not be different enough from half of one outlaw's gold. The tracks would not be different enough to be able to tell which was which. Even so, for lack of any better idea, he mounted up and trotted over to where one double trail had left the area. He followed that trail for nearly a quarter of a mile, turned around to go back, when Val's voice carried on the wind. 'Over here!'

He jammed the spurs into his horse's sides much harder than he intended. The horse leaped forward, running flat out in three jumps. He caught up with Val scarcely three minutes later.

'What'd you find?' he called out, well before he had advanced to where the Pinkerton detective sat his horse, waiting.

Silently, Val pointed at the ground.

Sawing on the reins to pull his horse to a stop, Dwight stared where the smaller man pointed. Caught in the edge of a clump of sage brush was a piece of beige lace. Dwight's heart leaped into his throat. He leaped from his horse and walked a swift circle around the sage brush. Then he followed the two sets of tracks for a ways, then turned and ran back. He picked up the piece of lace. It was heavily wrinkled, giving evidence that it had been tightly crushed before it found its way to where they had found it.

'Is that hers?' Val asked.

Dwight forced himself to be calm. He relived in his mind the picture of Mac holding the shotgun to the

101

base of Belinda's skull. He remembered the dress she was wearing. He looked at the lace. 'Yeah,' he said, the word catching in his throat.

'She marked her trail?' Val asked.

A mirthless smile spread across Dwight's face. 'Sure's anything. She found a way to let me know which set o' tracks was hers.'

Not wasting the time to ask if that were the set of tracks Dwight would be following, Val said, 'I would guess that Bandy will be one of the other double set of tracks. He would most certainly commandeer one of the extra horses to aid his getaway. I have a fifty-fifty chance of guessing the right one. Since he was overseeing the division of the loot, that would most likely mean he was one of the last to leave. I will guess it to be the other set of tracks that lead just a little way west from the set you'll be following.'

'Makes sense,' Dwight agreed, already back in the saddle.

'I'll mark these two trails,' Val offered. 'That way the rest of them will know which ones to follow and which ones we are already pursuing.'

Dwight nodded, impatient to be moving.

'They will be more easily caught than they realize,' he assured Dwight.

Dwight frowned. 'Why's that?'

Val smiled. 'I'm sure none of them has ever seen that much gold, let alone tried to transport it. It is amazingly heavy. If it doesn't tear out the seams of their saddle-bags, it will tire their horses much, much more quickly than they expect. They will either push their horses too hard and exhaust them quickly, or they will have to travel slowly enough to be readily overtaken.'

'Except the two with a spare horse.'

'Except the two with a spare horse,' Val echoed.

Dwight didn't wait to hear any more. He didn't wait to watch Val scratch arrows in the dirt pointing toward the tracks they each followed. He didn't see him scratch a 'V L' beside one arrow, and a 'D S' beside the other. He didn't look back to see the dust cloud rapidly approaching from town, as the posse raced to take up the pursuit. All he could see was the image of the woman he loved in the grasp of the outlaw.

He didn't realize the amount of attention he was paying to the trail of the two horses. He was a consummate tracker. He had tracked so many people so many miles; he watched for the telltale broken blades of grass, the stones kicked out of where they had lain, the occasional faint impression of a horse's hoof, or the broken small branch of a clump of sage or a smashed branch of a bush, as if it were instinctive to him.

He urged his horse to a rapid trot. After the first quarter of a mile, it seemed as if the horse himself recognized the trail they were following. Whether he saw the same things his rider saw, or whether he could still smell the other horses, didn't really matter. He was now every bit as much a pursuer as his master.

Stern's eyes covered every inch of the ground ahead and beside the trail he followed. He spotted the next piece of lace well before they got to it, as it fluttered in the breeze. He didn't stop to look at it. He just offered a silent prayer that Mac would not catch her leaving the telltale sign.

Every time he approached the crest of a hill he drew his horse to a walk, removed his hat, and stood as high in the stirrups as he could. When he was just near enough to see over the top of whatever rise lay before him, he reined the horse to a stop and studied the land ahead.

'He either knows the country or he's scouted it out real well,' he told his ever-attentive horse. 'He's givin' a wide berth to every minin' camp an' town.'

The sun rose to its zenith and began its slow descent toward the distant mountains. Sweat streaked the flanks of his horse. He had long since removed his vest and rolled it behind the saddle, tying it into place with a couple of the strings attached to the saddle. His shirt was soaked with sweat.

Twice, as they crossed a small trickle of water from a spring, he stopped and let the horse drink his fill. Each time he refilled his canteen, poured water over his head and torso, filled the canteen again, and continued on the trail.

At the first place he stopped at he noted with a strange mixture of irritation and pleasure that Mac had not afforded either his horses or his captive an opportunity to drink. That meant Belinda was more than likely miserable with thirst. On the other hand, it also meant he was reducing their horses' endurance.

At the second place he stopped for his horse to drink, he brought out a bag of oats from one of his saddle-bags. He poured a measure of them into his hat and allowed the horse to eat them. He was going to do everything he knew to stretch the endurance of his own mount.

Darkness settled on to the land just as he came to yet another place to water his horse. He let him rest a while and fed him another handful of oats. He knew there should be a good enough moon to be able to follow the trail as soon as it rose. That gave him and his horse almost two hours to rest. He slipped the bit from his horse's mouth and picketed him in a patch of tall grass, within reach of the tiny rivulet of water. He lay down without benefit of a blanket. He forced all thoughts of Belinda and the mental turmoil that churned within him aside, willing himself to go to sleep. He'd had almost no sleep the night before, worrying about the possibility of exactly what had happened. Now the edge of his agitation had been worn away by the long day in the saddle, and the conviction that he was gaining on those he pursued. He knew he needed all the strength and endurance he could muster. By long practice and discipline, he actually managed to drop off to sleep.

# CHAPTER 14

The cloud of dust wasn't really a cloud at all. It was closer to a puff. Just a wisp of dust quickly borne away by the ceaseless wind. It was enough. A tight smile formed on Dwight's face, cracking the crust of dried sweat and dirt that masked him. The day of reckoning had come.

He nudged his tired horse into a trot, dropping quickly off the top of the rolling hill from which he had spotted the first sign of his quarry. They were not far ahead! He knew from their tracks that their horses were near exhaustion. Whether Mac knew, or only suspected, that he was hot on his trail, he was pushing the animals far too hard.

When he first began trailing them, Dwight recognized he was falling farther and farther behind those he pursued. He resisted the urge to demand greater speed from his own mount. Then the trail ceased to be growing older, as their pace slowed to match his own. The carefully measured tread he had disciplined himself to maintain finally began to pay off.

The farther he had come, the fresher their trail became.

He glanced at the sky. The brazen sun announced the approach of midday. Yesterday's sweat on man and beast had dried with the setting sun, then changed to a distinct chill with the dropping temperature of the night. Now fresh sweat dissolved anew the coating of dust and grime of yesterday, adding another wet layer of briny dirt coating both man and animal.

He had slept for just over an hour while waiting for the moon to rise. When it did, the soft light it lavished on the land woke him at once. He fed his horse another bait of oats from the saddle-bag. Then they resumed his dogged quest to overtake the fugitive and his hostage.

He favored his own hunger with a couple dried biscuits and a chunk of jerky, washed down with carefully measured amounts of water from his canteen as he rode.

At sunup he found another seep spring. He stopped and refilled his canteen, and refreshed himself and the horse, and set out once again.

Excitement welled up within him at the realization that his prey was almost within reach.

Three hours later he lay at the top of a ridge fifty yards to the side of the path his quarry followed. He had turned aside and ridden faster than he had previously dared. Now he watched as they approached a water hole that was little more than a large puddle in the bottom of a long draw. The horses walked woodenly, heads down, ears back, oblivious to everything around them. It was instantly obvious to him the animals were at the limit of their endurance.

From his vantage point, Dwight could see there was better water 200 yards down the shallow gully. From their location it remained hidden.

His face a mask devoid of expression, he backed off the ridge and trotted to his horse. He reined him around and rode as swiftly as he dared to the far side of a ridge that shielded him from their view. He slid out of the saddle, rifle in hand, and crawled silently to the top of the ridge. He removed his hat, crept up behind a clump of soap weed, and peered carefully around its base.

Less than a hundred yards away Mac and Belinda lay on their stomachs, drinking thirstily from the murky brown water.

Sighting along the rifle barrel, Dwight considered dispatching the outlaw without warning. His finger tightened on the trigger. He held his breath. He willed the finger to pull the trigger. It failed to respond. Whether it was wise or foolish, he could not bring himself to shoot even that man in cold blood.

Instead he yelled, 'Throw up your hands!'

Some part of his mind was aware of Belinda's squeal of delight, as she instantly recognized his voice.

The rest of his mind was riveted on Mac. He sprang from his prone position with stunning agility. Dwight's bullet kicked dirt and mud into the water hole from where the outlaw had been an instant before.

Mac's pistol was in his hand, spitting fire. Dirt kicked up inches to Dwight's right, then again, closer. All the while the outlaw was sprinting toward his horse. Dwight levered a second round into the chamber and squeezed the trigger of his rifle again. Mac flinched and swore, returning Dwight's fire yet again, but well wide of the mark.

Mac stepped into the left stirrup of his mount, but did not swing aboard. Instead he yelled at the startled horse, and fired another round at Dwight over the top of the saddle. The horse leaped forward in spite of its extreme fatigue, giving every ounce of its heart to a master who didn't deserve any part of its loyalty.

Staying all but completely out of sight behind his horse, Mac sprinted for the cover of a curve in the draw. Dwight considered shooting the horse, but didn't have the heart to do so. In seconds Mac was out of sight behind a hogback that jutted into the gully.

'Stay down!' Dwight yelled at Belinda as he ran in the direction his quarry had fled. When he rounded the corner behind which the outlaw had disappeared a warning screamed in his mind. He dropped flat on the ground, even as he heard the angry buzz of a leaden projectile passing over his head. He had an instant's glimpse of the outlaw then, as he disappeared over the lip of the draw.

Leaping to his feet, Dwight sprinted to the top of the gully, hoping for at least a long shot. Almost 200 yards away he caught one glimpse of color as it disappeared into brush and rocks. He stood and watched a long moment. He was certain he had at least nicked the outlaw. He was equally certain the man's horse could not carry him far. If he kept him moving at that pace, the animal would drop dead within a mile. If he allowed him to slow, he might carry the rider a goodly distance. That Mac would ride him until he dropped, with no qualms, he was certain.

He turned and hurried back to where Belinda waited. She stood as still as Lot's wife until Dwight was half a dozen steps from her. Then she uttered a squeak that sounded almost bestial, and lunged toward him. He dropped his rifle and wrapped his arms around her.

He waited for her to lift her face to him, but she failed to do so. It took several seconds for him to realize she was leaning heavily against him. Whether from exhaustion or relief, she was unable to stand erect. He held her tightly, his own voice more of a croak than a croon, as he said, over and over, 'It's all right, darling. It's all right. I'm here. I've been following you. It's all right. I wouldn't let him have you. It's all right now. You know I would never let him have you. It's all right. You're safe now.'

It was fully three minutes before she uttered a sound. It was a sob that first broke through. It jerked her whole body as it forced its way up through the walls of her stubborn resolve. It shattered that resolve as it erupted. With the barriers broken, her fear and anger and hunger and thirst and fatigue all surged forth in a loud, broken wail. She kept trying to talk, to pour out to Dwight all the pent-up feelings of the past two days, but he couldn't understand a single word she said. Not knowing what else to do, he simply held her, turning himself and her around so he could watch the direction in which Mac had fled, just in case he decided to double back.

At last she grew silent. The immediacy of her emotion spent, Belinda looked up into his face for the first time. She knew the tired lines around his eyes, the caked dirt on his face, the stale sweat that soaked him, were a mirror of her own condition. It didn't matter in the least. She grasped him by the back of the head, pulling his face down to hers. She kissed him hard, fiercely, frantically, as if only that could convey to him the relief and gratitude that flooded through her. Neither was in the least mindful of the caked dirt and mud they shared in that moment.

Eventually she collected herself enough to straighten and step back slightly. Her voice broke as she said, 'Did you . . . is he. . . ?'

Dwight shook his head. 'I think I nicked him. I don't know how good. He won't get far, spent as his horse is.'

'Will . . . will he come back?'

Dwight considered it. He chewed his upper lip, surprised at the amount of dirt his teeth came back with. He spat on to the ground. He shook his head. 'I dunno. He might. He might just decide all that money he's got is enough.'

Belinda shook her head. 'He won't. He put most of it in my saddle-bags and tied it into the bedroll on the horse I rode. He said I only weighed half what he did, so that'd balance the load better.'

'He didn't even stop to let the horses rest last night, did he?'

'He didn't even slow down,' she confirmed. 'He was like a man possessed. He was sure you'd be right behind us. So was I, darling. I just knew you'd come. I just knew it. The only reason I kept going along with him, instead of trying to make a run for it, was that I knew you'd be coming.'

'There wasn't much else you could do.'

'I felt so helpless when he grabbed me in town.'

'You were. So were we. He had that rigged up real good, so nobody'd dare take a shot at him. Even if I'd shot 'im in the head, his thumbs would've come off them hammers and fired the shotgun.'

She shuddered at the thought that had haunted her since the moment Mac had grabbed her. 'I just don't know what I could've done,' she said again.

'There wasn't anything,' he reassured her.

She wasn't content to leave it like that, however. 'There must have been something I could have done to give you a chance, at least.'

He thought about it a long moment. 'The only thing you could've done would've had to be set up ahead o' time. If we'da had some code word or some-thin' . . . you know, like if I said "drop". Then you'd know to just drop, like you was faintin' or somethin'. Just go plumb limp. If we'da had somethin' like that

112

set up, and I coulda distracted 'im, made him move the shotgun a little bit for just a second, then I coulda hollered, you coulda dropped, and I mighta had a chance to shoot 'im. That's way too many ifs. Anyway, we didn't never have no idea o' nothin' like that happenin', so there's no way we'da had somethin' like that set up ahead o' time. So there just wasn't nothin' you coulda done. But it's all right. I got you back, and Mac's on the run. It'll be OK now.'

It seemed the appropriate time for another kiss. This time they both noticed the amount of dirt they shared in the process. As if acting on the same impulse, they both wiped their mouths with the backs of their hands as they parted. Belinda giggled. Then she couldn't stop giggling. She nearly fell, but leaned against him, trying to stifle the uncontrollable urge. When she could do so sufficiently to talk, she accused him, 'You wiped my kiss off!'

He grinned. 'Naw. I wiped the dirt off, but I left the kiss on OK. You are one dirty woman, though. Do you ever take a bath?'

She didn't respond. Her mood swung abruptly again. Her eyes widened with sudden terror. 'He will come back, won't he?'

'I 'spect so,' Dwight admitted. 'Are you able to ride a while longer? We can't stay here.'

She looked around, casting fearful glances in all directions. 'I'll have to. We have to get out of here,' she agreed.

Dwight had left his own horse over the top of the ridge at the edge of the draw. Suddenly ashamed he

113

had left him that long within the smell of water, but bound by training to stay put, he turned his head and tried to whistle. All that came out was a dry whoosh of sound. He wiped his hand across his mouth again, licked his lips, and tried again. This time it worked.

Almost instantly his horse appeared, holding his head to one side to avoid stepping on the trailing reins. He slid and skidded down the side of the gully and went directly to the water hole.

'He looks so much better than my horse,' Belinda said.

Dwight nodded. 'I been grainin' 'im an' keepin' 'im watered halfway decent. He's wearin' down pretty bad, though.'

'Let's get out of here,' she said, suddenly frantic to get away from where Mac knew them to be.

As they rode away Dwight led the way for nearly 300 yards. As they started, Belinda said, 'Why are we going this way?'

'Leavin' tracks,' was all he said.

When they reached a stretch of rocky shale, he turned at right angles. Carefully guiding the horses to where there was little or no trace of their passing, they rode for almost two miles. He found a shallow swale in the bottom of a large draw that was surrounded by trees and brush. They would be invisible there from any distance greater than fifty yards. In the trees twenty yards farther on, a tiny brook flowed softly between banks of tall grass.

He removed the saddles and bridles from their horses. As he slid the saddle from Belinda's horse, it slipped from his hands and fell to the ground. 'Wow!' he said softly. 'That's heavy!'

He led the horses to the tiny creek and picketed them there, where they could reach all the grass and water they could want.

Returning to the small clearing, he removed the bedroll from his own saddle and the saddle-bags and bedroll both from Belinda's. Marveling again at the weight of them, he hid them in the brush at the edge of the clearing. Then he took his bedroll and spread his blankets just outside the open area, on the other side of the clearing. They would be invisible to anyone walking into the clearing, but he had only to open his eyes to see across its expanse.

Wordlessly he laid down on his blankets. Belinda collapsed beside him and leaned back against him. He put an arm around her, pulling a blanket over the both of them. He stayed awake just long enough to enjoy the feel of her body against him for a few minutes. She was already asleep before that.

# CHAPTER 15

Dwight's eyes opened abruptly, wide and alert. Tired as he was, sleepiness fled to some distant chamber of his well-disciplined mind. He quietly slid his arm up from where it rested across Belinda's waist. He clamped his hand over her mouth.

Belinda jumped, grabbing at the hand stifling any sound she might make.

'Shh,' Dwight whispered into her ear. 'Stay real quiet.'

Belinda relaxed as awareness returned, and she realized it was Dwight who was silencing her. She turned her head, seeking his face in the deep darkness, but unable to see anything.

With his mouth against her ear, Dwight breathed, 'Somebody's out there. The horses are movin'. Stay here an' don't move.'

Silent as a shadow he slid from beneath the blanket that covered them both. Stocking-footed, gun in hand, he crept slowly through the trees toward where he had picketed their horses.

The moon had set, casting the earth into deep blackness. He knew it had to be within an hour or two of dawn. Whoever was out there was trying hard to make no noise, so it had to be either Indians, or Mac had backtracked and found them.

He eased from tree to tree, straining to see, to hear, to sense the presence of another. Cautious as he was, he rustled a clump of dried leaves that had blown up against the twig of a bush sprouting from the fertile ground. Instantly a gun roared. Twice in rapid succession, fingers of fire reached out for him from the darkness.

Both shots missed, but barely. He responded instantly. He fired once directly at the flashes of fire and swiftly to either side. Even as he fired he moved quickly to the side, lest whoever was out there return fire at his gun flashes.

No sound of a bullet thwacking into flesh rewarded his effort. He did, however, hear the sound of rapid movement as someone beat a hasty retreat.

He stood where he was for a long moment, listening. The silence of the night settled around him again, carrying no information, no warning, no reassurance.

As silently as possible he ejected the spent brass from his gun and replaced the spaces in the cylinder with fresh shells from his cartridge belt.

Once again he began to move, slowly and carefully, placing each foot down only after he had felt the ground with it, ensuring his weight would not create sound that would make him a target.

117

He came to the edge of the trees, yards from where he had picketed the horses. He listened for their breathing, for the shuffle of their feet, for the sound of their teeth tearing at the grass, for any huff of recognition from either of them. He heard nothing. Heart pounding at the thought of being exposed and vulnerable, he moved stealthily out of the timber. He already knew what he would find. If the horses had been where he had left them, he would have already heard them, sensed them. If nothing more, they would have responded to his presence. They were gone.

Sudden fear for Belinda's safety shot through him. What if whoever it was had circled around and had already discovered her?

Moving more swiftly than silently, he retraced his steps, stopping twenty feet from the blankets he had so recently slid out of. He listened intently. He heard nothing.

Softly, carefully, he said, 'Belinda?' then swiftly stepped three steps sideways.

A soft voice responded. 'Dwight?'

Relief flooded through him. 'You OK?'

'Yes. What happened?'

'Somebody found us.'

'Who?'

'Don't know. Mac, is my guess.'

'You didn't get him?'

'Don't think so. Too dark to be sure. The horses are gone.'

She gasped. 'He took the horses?'

'Don't think so. I came close enough to 'im that he lit a shuck. I'da heard the horses if he had 'em.'

'He just turned them loose?'

'That's my guess. Maybe not deliberate. Mighta had 'em loose, and he had to leave 'em when I showed up. Stop talkin' now. He might be listenin'. We gotta move.'

Following the sound of her voice, he had moved beside her as they talked. He noticed with approval that she had moved some distance from their blankets, against his instructions, and had hidden. Taking her hand, he led her quietly through the brush and timber to a spot against a sheer bank that rose twenty feet into the air at the edge of the draw. He sat down, his back against the bank, to await the dawn. A small field of large boulders lay between them and the rest of the draw.

Taking her cue from him, she eased down beside him, leaned against him, and fell back asleep almost instantly.

He didn't stir until the pink fingers of dawn touched their artistic brush across the bottoms of the scattered clouds, turning them into orange and crimson canvasses of gorgeous light and color. He studied the area around them carefully, watching for any hint of motion. There was none.

He studied the area where they had hidden their saddles and the loot Mac had loaded on to Belinda's horse. Nothing seemed disturbed.

He moved then, wakening Belinda instantly. Her eyes jerked open wide, filled with fear. She grasped

119

his arm, her head swiveling this way and that. 'It's OK,' Dwight said softly. 'It's comin' daylight. I gotta go look around.'

She straightened, twisting her shoulders to relieve the stiff muscles of her back and arms. 'Can you find the horses?'

He nodded. 'Should be able to. They ain't apt to go far from that crick an' all the good grass, bein' as tired an' hungry as they were.'

'What about Mac? Do you think that's who it was?'

'Just about gotta be. Indians woulda made a circle an' waited for daylight. We'd already be gettin' a message from 'em if that was the case.'

She shuddered at the thought. Before she had a chance to answer, Dwight said, 'Here's my rifle and a box o' shells. Stay right here an' keep a sharp eye out. If anyone comes along, you can lie down behind them big rocks an' hold 'em off till kingdom come. Nobody can get around behind you here, on account o' the bank.'

'Where are you going?'

'I gotta see if I can follow Mac. Then I gotta catch up to them horses. We're dead out here without horses. But I gotta take care o' Mac first.'

'Maybe he's gone. Maybe he just chased off our horses and left us to die trying to walk out of here.'

He shook his head. 'He ain't goin' anywhere without all that gold an' money in your saddle-bags. He wants you plumb bad, too. He trailed us back here to get it an' get you, an' he won't quit till he has both or he has a chunk o' lead in 'im.'

120

Without waiting for an answer, he stood up and walked to where the blankets were still spread on the ground. He picked up each of his boots, shook them upside down one at a time, to be sure nothing had crawled into them during the night. As he shook the second one, the distinct sound of a rattlesnake's rattle emitted from it. He swore and threw the boot. As soon as it landed, a timber rattler crawled out and disappeared into the brush. His gun was in his hand even before it appeared, but he held his fire. Shooting the snake would instantly telegraph his position to Mac, assuming he was waiting and watching. He shook the boot again, and put it on. It took him several minutes to recover his concentration and for his heart to stop hammering in his chest.

He had spent the intervening time since his discovery of the missing horses thinking about what the outlaw would most likely do. It seemed the best bet that he would circle the spot where he knew they were, and watch for a chance to dry-gulch them. He headed for the spot where he last knew the outlaw to be, the spot from which the shots in the darkness had come.

'He's gotta figure I'll go there an' start trackin' 'im,' he told himself silently, 'so he'll be where he can get a pot-shot at me when I do.'

He studied the area surrounding them in the growing light. His eyes kept coming back to a high spot that had resisted the erosion that created the rest of the draw. It would be a perfect spot for someone to lie in ambush.

121

Keeping out of sight of that spot, he used the timber and brush as cover, working his way to the edge of the draw. He climbed the gentle slope it boasted at that spot. Halfway up the side he spotted Mac's horse, cropping grass and eating as best he could with the bridle bit still in his mouth. Hoping the horse was too tired and too hungry to be concerned about his presence, he worked his way toward the vantage point he sought. He emerged at that lip of the ravine less than a dozen yards from the spot on which he had set his sights.

He was rewarded instantly. Lying prone on the rock-strewn crest of the rise, Jarvis McCrae watched the area where Dwight and Belinda had spent the night. Gun in hand, Dwight said, 'Watchin' for me?'

Mac whirled, firing as he turned. The shot went wide. Even as he fired, Mac dived sideways, tucked his shoulder, rolled once and came to his feet. Dwight's own shot pursued him, but failed to connect.

As Mac came to his feet he fired again at Dwight, the bullet tugging gently at his hat.

Dwight returned the shot, but swore even as he squeezed the trigger. Mac had disappeared. It seemed as if he had disappeared into thin air. Seconds later Dwight heard the outlaw's horse retreat down the draw.

Dwight slid down the side of the gully, then climbed the gentle knoll to where the outlaw had lain in wait. From the marks on the ground it was apparent he had been there since being shot at by

Dwight the night before.

'Had his spot all picked out, so he could go right to it in the dark,' he marveled. 'Doesn't that man ever need to sleep?'

It took him the better part of an hour to find their horses. Following the easy trail they had left in the tall grass along the creek, he whistled softly for his own mount. The horse trotted to him at once. He swung astride him bareback, knowing Belinda's would follow the other horse.

He had scarcely started back toward where he had left her when he heard the bark of her rifle, followed almost at once by three more shots.

Swearing, he kicked his reluctant mount into a trot. Just short of the spot he had picketed them the night before, he stopped and slid from the horse's back. Hoping they wouldn't stray again, he had no choice but to leave them and hurry to her rescue.

Belinda's rifle barked again. There was no answering fire.

Frowning, Dwight moved as swiftly as he could without making noise. He ascended the side of the draw, aiming for a spot above the cliff where he had left her. He was nearly there when an Indian rose from the brush and walked to the edge of that cliff. As he raised his rifle, aiming downward, Dwight fired twice in rapid succession. The Indian yelled, dropped his rifle, threw his hands upward, and toppled off the edge of the low cliff.

Scrambling on hands and knees, Dwight approached the drop-off. He could clearly see

Belinda below. She was still lying behind the cover where he had left her, but she was twisted around, her eyes searching for whomever was behind and above her.

Twice Dwight caught a slight glimpse of movement, going away from them. In moments the drumbeat of three horses retreated into the distance.

'Are you OK?' he called to Belinda.

'Yes. Did you get him?'

'Mac?'

'Yes.'

'No. He got to his horse and took off again. The Indians must've heard me shoot, and started lookin'. They spotted you instead o' me, 'cause I was gone after our horses.'

'Did you get them?'

'Yeah. I might have to catch 'em again, though. They ain't tied or nothin'.'

'I think I shot one of the Indians. Maybe two.'

As they talked, he walked along the edge of the gully until he found a spot where he could slide down. She rushed into his arms. 'Oh, Dwight, I was so scared! I never even heard them coming, but I saw something move, and was watching. I figured out it was Indians, and when I had a clear shot, I shot at one. He went down, and the others shot back at me. They came close enough for chips of rock to hit me in the face. Then there was nothing. Just . . . nothing. I watched and listened, and couldn't see or hear anything. Then I saw the grass moving, and shot where it was moving. I think I might have hit that one too.

It sounded like the bullet hit something, anyway. Then you shot the one that had circled around above me. He would have killed me before I even knew he was there.'

As she talked, her arms around him, the side of her face against his chest, her shaking slowly subsided. 'You did good,' he said. 'You did real good. But we need to get the horses saddled and get out of here. Those Indians might be back with others before long. They'll sure be comin' back to try to collect their dead.'

'But Mac is still out there, somewhere?'

'He's still out there.'

'He won't stop chasing us until he's dead, will he?'

'Not likely.'

She shuddered. 'Are we ever going to just be safe again?'

He wanted to assure her that Mac had ridden away and they were already safe. He just wasn't that good a liar. He well knew it was still a long way back to Headland. He also knew the man who pursued them was an absolute madman.

# CHAPTER 16

It was just called 'Kelly's Draw'. It was uncertain whether anyone even knew who 'Kelly' was, or why the tawdry mining camp bore his name.

It wasn't anything too many folks would have been proud to see bearing their name. It was made up of tents, hastily assembled shacks, a few overused out-houses, and an occasional open-fronted lean-to, selling essentials for the survival of hopeful miners and prospectors.

The single street of the camp was beaten to fine powder by countless hoofs of horses, mules, and a rare milk cow or ox. 'The first time it rains, that street's gonna be belly deep in mud,' Dwight observed.

He hadn't wanted to even pass through the camp. He just didn't feel that they had a choice. Since their scrape with the Indians, he and Belinda had taken a circuitous course rather than head straight back toward Headland. Their horses were jaded. They had far too much weight to carry, given the amount of gold that still burdened Belinda's saddle-bags and bedroll. They were out of any kind of food, other than the one cottontail rabbit Dwight had shot. He was out of oats for the horses, and unless they stopped for a complete day and night to allow the animals to rest and eat they would give out. They really needed to have oats as well, to keep them going until they got back to Headland.

They were dead tired. Afraid to sleep and too exhausted not to sleep, they had managed to catch an hour or two of fitful sleep only rarely.

He pocketed some of the paper money that belonged to the bank, making a careful note in his tally book of the amount. Whatever they could find at the mining camp would be three or four times a fair price, but they couldn't afford to quibble. Neither could anyone else. That was why everything sold for three or four times its fair price.

Although there was nothing approaching a permanent building, Dwight quickly counted five saloons along the street. They consisted of little more than planks on upended whiskey barrels, behind which the owner dispensed the liquid that seemed to be more important than food.

At the end of the street a pair of freight wagons had a similar plank – this one supported by two large boulders that had been rolled into place – behind which two men offered assorted items of clothing, picks, shovels, ropes, dynamite and fuses, and whatever else might lie hidden beneath the tarpaulins that covered the contents of the wagons. They seemed to be doing a brisk business.

A little ways down the street, sandwiched between two places selling whiskey, another wagon sold food-stuffs from its tailgate. As they stopped at that wagon, Belinda said, 'You haven't even unhitched your horses!'

The man with the wagon said, 'No need, lady. My boy's givin' 'em feed an' water where they stand. I'll be sold out afore the day's over and headin' back for another load.'

Dwight's attention was suddenly arrested by a loud voice, back a little ways from the street, a little farther down the narrow gulch. 'Days of judgment are upon us,' the voice declared in stentorian tones. 'It is time to repent and seek the forgiveness of a merciful God, for he will not long abide the vices and excesses of this pit of iniquity. Unless there is great repentance, the fate of Sodom and Gomorrah will descend upon you. The Word of God will be pro-claimed from this location two hours from now, before the sun goes down. Come one, come all, and give your sinful souls an opportunity to seek God's grace while you can.'

'Bandy!' Dwight breathed. 'Can you beat that! He's right there in front of us, hidin' in plain sight.'

'Is that the man who drove the wagon?' Belinda marveled.

'That's him,' Dwight affirmed. 'All dolled up in that broadcloth suit an' preacher's collar, figgerin' nobody's gonna recognize 'im, or even think to look here for 'im.'

'He rode straight here,' a voice at Dwight's shoulder said.

Dwight whirled. Val Lindquist stood directly behind them. 'Where'd you come from?' Dwight demanded.

'Virginia, originally,' Val replied with a perfectly straight face.

'Long ride,' Dwight responded just as soberly. 'You must not've stopped to sleep much.'

'You two don't look like you've had a lot of sleep either,' Lindquist observed. 'I see you caught up with McCrae.'

Dwight's eyes turned hard. 'I got Belinda back. I didn't get McCrae. Mighta nicked him once, but I missed every other shot I had at him.'

'He'll show up,' Val observed.

'Here?'

'Count on it.'

'What's goin' on? How come you ain't nailed Bandy?'

'He has his share of the loot hidden. Frank Singler and Harvey Frieden are here as well. The one they were tracking rode in the opposite direction for a ways, then turned and rode directly toward here. They lost his trail in all the other tracks about five miles from here.'

'They rode here?'

Val nodded. 'As did Bandy. As did also Johnny Rivers.'

'Who's trackin' him?'

'Howard Glendenning and a cowboy from the

Muleshoe Ranch, who is a tracker.'

'And Rivers came here?'

'It would seem so. As with the one Frank and Harvey tracked. They all rode a false direction for a little ways, then came directly here. It would be very surprising if McCrae doesn't show up here as well. All who are here are keeping well out of sight. None of us has spotted any of them. Only Bandy is hiding in the open, presuming nobody will recognize him in his role as a preacher.'

'So how come you ain't nailed Bandy?'

'He does not have his share of the loot with him. Neither, so far as we can tell, do the others. None of them is spending any of it at any of the saloons, which is amazing, to say the least. The only way to recover it is to watch and wait.'

'Watch and wait for what?'

'For whomever is behind the entire plan.'

'I thought that was Bandy.'

'It has Bandy who was supervising everything. It is not likely he is behind it.'

'Why not?'

'Because neither he nor any of the others has any way to dispose of that much gold. You cannot just walk into a bank with a thousand pounds of gold and make a deposit. Somebody has to be behind it who has a way to do that.'

The thought had never occurred to Dwight. He found himself with his mouth open, staring at the smaller man.

'That makes sense,' Belinda offered.

Dwight closed his mouth and took off his hat. He ran a hand through his hair, then put his hat back on. 'You gotta be right,' he acknowledged. 'I guess I ain't thinkin' too good. We gotta find a place that's safe to rest up and rest our horses. We've been afraid to go to sleep the whole time, and our horses are plumb shot.'

'Those of the posse who have arrived here have set up a camp of sorts a little way outside of town. I will lead you there when we can be sure you have not been spotted and are not being followed. We maintain the appearance of place miners to allay suspicion. We keep a guard posted at all times, so you will be able to rest.'

Those were the sweetest words either Dwight or Belinda had heard in what seemed like a very long time.

# CHAPTER 17

The prospect of being able to relax and sleep was like something out of an impossible dream. Even so, Dwight silently lamented the necessity of him and Belinda not being able to share their blankets, as necessity had prompted since her rescue. Now, as during that time, their utter exhaustion precluded anything but sleep, but her closeness had been unutterably precious to him. He had admitted to himself that he never wanted to sleep again without being able to feel her next to him.

In the camp with the others of the impromptu posse, that was, of course, impossible. He would do nothing to stain her reputation. He was not too exhausted to tease her a bit, however.

'How are we gonna sleep together with all these other folks around?'

Her eyes danced as she feigned umbrage. 'We're not, that's how. In fact, how dare you even suggest we share a bed, yet! If you want me in your bed, you can jolly well put a ring on my finger.'

'That didn't seem to bother you since I caught up with you'n McCrae.'

'That was different, and you know it! That was just a necessity for what sleep we could manage. That's not at all the same as planning to sleep for the night.'

'Well, we could just go ahead and get married, I 'spect.'

'And how do you propose to do that in this makeshift mining camp?'

'There's a preacher here. That's all we need.'

'A preacher? Here?'

'Bandy's a preacher. Ordained, bona fide, genuine as they come!'

Eyes still sparkling, she called his bluff instantly. 'Wonderful! Let's just march over there to where he has his revival tent set up and ask him to perform the ceremony.'

Dwight opened his mouth and closed it again. He took off his hat, ran his hand through his hair, scratched the back of his neck, put the hat back on and cleared his throat. 'Well, the only problem with that is that he'd sure as sin shoot me on sight. Or I'd have to shoot him. Either one would make it kinda hard for me to say "I do".'

'Maybe he'd consent to delay the shooting part until after the "I do"?'

'But then you might just have a dead husband.'

'At least I'd have a husband. All I've managed so far is a promise of "one of these fine days" that never seems to come.'

He instantly lost all semblance of joviality. His eyes

took on a pained look. 'Honey, you know that ain't fair! All I been waitin' for is to have a decent place for you to live, before we tie the knot.'

Her voice took on an unaccustomed edge. 'And all I've been waiting for is for you to stop making excuses! I've already told you I'd be happy to share a tent in a cactus patch with you, if that's all we have.'

He again went through his routine of removing his hat, running a hand through his hair, scratching the back of his neck, and putting the hat back on. 'I'm sorry,' he said. 'I thought you was willin' to wait a bit longer.'

'Well, I'm not.' Her voice was flat. A spark of deep anger and hurt shone through the usual control of her gaze. She was simply too exhausted to pretend, or to conceal her emotions. 'I feel like I'm just being strung along, stalled, pushed aside, wanted but not really wanted, and I'm tired of it, Dwight. I'm tired of it. When we get back to Headland, either we get married or you can go find someone else to make excuses to.'

He stood with his mouth open, stunned at the depth of her hurt and anger over his continuing postponement of their wedding. 'But . . . but . . . but I've told you time and again that I'm totally committed to you!'

'But you're not!' she shot back. 'Words are cheap. Commitment is a ring, Dwight. As long as I don't have a ring on this finger,' she held up her left hand, 'there is no commitment. I want to be your wife, not just the woman held in thrall by your endless hot air promises, always and forever waiting for a real, tangible commitment.'

Again he stared at her, at a total loss for words. Then he said, again, 'I'm sorry. I ain't been seein' it that way. We'll get married just as soon as we get back to town.'

'Thank you,' she said, suddenly too far spent even to talk any longer. 'I have to get to sleep now. I'm about ready to collapse.'

He stepped forward and put his arms around her. She leaned against him, but did not return his embrace. He said, 'I put our blankets over there, so's we'd be as close together as I figured would be seemly.'

Without a word she walked away from him. She lowered herself to the blankets, pulled off her shoes, covered herself and turned on her side, her back toward the blankets he had arranged for himself. She was asleep in less than two minutes.

He was not so fortunate. He lay in the fading light of the early evening, her words, '... either we get married or you can go find someone else to make excuses to,' kept echoing over and over in his mind.

He stared at her back, so close to him but suddenly so very far away. The thought that he might lose her left a hollow feeling in the middle of his stomach that physically hurt. 'I really didn't know,' he said silently, half a dozen times, before his own fatigue wrapped a soothing cloak of sleep around everything.

# CHAPTER 18

Dwight woke with a start. He sat up, his gun in his hand as if of its own volition.

The moon hung low over the nearby mountain. In the deep shadows formed by its soft glow he made out the forms of sleeping men. His darting eyes picked out the darker shadow of the sentry, sitting at the base of a tree.

At first he thought the sentry was asleep or dead, then the man moved. His head turned slowly from side to side, scanning all approaches to the posse's hidden campsite.

Memory rushed through the fog of Dwight's fatigue. He remembered where he was, and that he was safe, at least for the moment.

He turned toward Belinda's blankets, a few feet away. She still lay as she had when she first fell asleep, her back turned toward him. The rise and fall of her regular breathing attested to the soundness of her sleep.

He lay back down, placing his gun once again at his side, beneath the blankets. He stared at Belinda's blanketed back until he dropped off to sleep again.

His eyes jerked open to that same soft glow of light. It took him a moment to realize it was no longer moonlight, but the first light of a new day that had wakened him. That he had relaxed enough to sleep the night through amazed him.

He looked over at Belinda's blankets, noting that at some time during the night she had turned to face him, but she was still sound asleep.

His eyes moved slowly around the campsite. Three of the posse were already up and moving. A small fire had been started, and a coffee pot rested in the coals at its edge. The smell of its contents just coming to a boil evoked an instant and powerful craving in him.

He rose silently from his blankets, sliding his gun into its holster as he did so. Going automatically through the ritual of shaking out his boots, he pulled them on. He strode to the fire.

Even as he did, other members of the posse were wakened by the smell of fresh coffee wafting on the slight breeze. It was quickly followed by the smell of frying side pork. With a stout stick, David Lowenberg lifted a Dutch oven from where it had been nearly buried in coals. *Must've been up for over an hour already,* Dwight mused silently.

He hadn't even noticed a second Dutch oven buried in the coals on the other side of the fire.

Together they held enough freshly baked biscuits to provide breakfast for the dozen men who quickly gathered around.

Dwight took one of the metal plates that was offered and a cup of the steaming black brew. Instead of eating, he carried it over to where Belinda remained asleep. With both hands full, he nudged her with a toe. Her eyes jerked open, wide with instant alarm. It took her a couple seconds to recognize Dwight, and her expression changed to misty-eyed relief. 'Oh, my!' she said, her eyes taking in the men busily eating breakfast. 'I must have really been sleeping!'

'You was sawin' logs pretty good,' he agreed. 'I brought you some breakfast.'

She started to reach for it, then realized she had a more urgent need. She looked around quickly, a look of near desperation crowding out everything else. Dwight nodded toward a thick clump of brush a dozen yards away, at the edge of the draw in which they were camped. She looked around again, almost fearfully, then slipped from the blankets and moved hurriedly out of sight behind the bushes. She emerged a few minutes later looking much relieved. 'Now I'd be happy to eat some of that breakfast,' she told him, a betraying tinge of red marking her cheeks.

They joined the others around the fire. As they approached, all the men stood and touched the brims of their hats, rather than removing them. A soft chorus of greetings briefly interrupted their busy devouring of the food.

Dwight managed to fill his own plate with what was nearly the last vestiges of the food. He washed it down with the more than ample quantity of coffee, however.

'How'd you get elected cook, Dave?' Dwight ribbed the owner of Headland's mercantile store.

'Cuz we wanted to be able to eat,' Harvey Frieden offered instantly. 'Frank cooked for us one meal, and that was enough.'

'Just tryin' to be economical,' Frank defended. 'If what I cooked was fit to eat, it'd cost a whole lot more to feed this bunch.'

'If I could charge as much for food as they do here, by golly I would feed you all for nothing,' Soren Swenson offered in his heavily accented voice.

'Fat chance, Soren,' Virgil Zucher rejoined. 'You'd decide it was worth too much money to waste on us, if that was the case.'

'Anybody seen Lindquist?' Ralph Humbolt interrupted the repartee.

As if on cue the Pinkerton detective strode in from the direction of the mining camp. 'Am I too late for breakfast?' he inquired.

Dave waved a hand toward the utensils at the fire's edge. 'There might be a chunk or two of side pork and one or two biscuits left,' he said.

Silently Val finished off what was left of the breakfast. Everybody patiently stared at him, waiting to see if there was any news. When he finished eating and had offered nothing, Frank said, 'Anything happenin' yet?'

Val nodded. 'A couple more of the gang have shown up. Tighson is one. I don't know the name of the other one, but he was there at the robbery.'

'How many's that make here now?'

'Six, that I've counted.'

'Must be gettin' close to time.'

Val looked meaningfully at Dwight and Belinda. 'Mac showed up this morning.'

Dwight pursed his lips. 'I'd have sworn I nicked him a time or two.'

Lindquist nodded. 'I would say you did. He is not moving very well. He's quite pale, and saying very little.'

'Not feelin' too good, huh?'

'He doesn't appear to be.'

'What about Bandy?'

'He is playing his role well. He doesn't give any hint that he knows any of his men when they show up. But well after dark they all get together at his tent.'

'Where he does his preachin'?'

Val nodded. 'He has a well-secluded section canvassed off behind where he preaches from. That's where he sleeps and such. The others slip in and out of there during the night. I gathered from the raised voices that some of them are getting more than a little impatient at the delay in whatever they are waiting for.'

'Which would be the mastermind of the whole shebang showin' up to pay 'em for the gold.'

'That would be my assumption.'

'He'll have to be bringin' a wagon,' Dwight observed.

Val nodded. 'But it's unlikely he will bring the wagon into the mining camp. An empty wagon arriving would excite too much attention and curiosity.'

'So he'll go directly to wherever they're keepin' the gold stashed.'

'Yes.'

'No idea where that is?'

Val's hesitancy was instantly obvious. After an awkward silence he said, 'As a matter of fact, I do have that location narrowed down quite a bit. I don't know exactly, but it has to be quite close.'

He had everybody's immediate attention. He picked up a stick and drew a quick map in the dirt. 'Here is the mining camp. This is the draw that opens up to the south and east about half a mile east of the camp itself. That's the opposite direction from all the paydirt anybody has discovered, so no one pays any attention to what goes on there. There is also a rather flat and easy access to that area from the east, which a team and wagon could navigate with relative ease.'

'But you haven't seen where they've got it stashed,' Dwight said, rather than asked.

Val shook his head. 'I have watched from a distance, with a spyglass. I believe it to be buried, and I believe I know to within a hundred yards of where, but I have not seen it. I think all of the gold has been brought in now, though.'

'Then we'd best be watchin' that spot right close,'

Frank observed.

Val nodded. 'As of today, that will be necessary. We will do that with two men watching from the lookout post I have been using at all times. Each team will man that post for eight hours or so before being relieved by another team.'

'Better make it three at a time,' Dwight suggested.

'Why three?'

'If somethin' starts happenin', one guy'll need to skedaddle back here an' get the rest, an' we'd best have at least two stayin' there.'

A murmur of agreement ran through the group. Val acknowledged the wisdom of the idea. 'That makes sense. At least one of us will need to keep an eye on Bandy at all times as well, without being seen by him or the others. That may be trickier, given the close confines of the mining camp.'

Soren Swenson spoke up. 'By golly, I know Keil Solinnen pretty well. He is the one that has the wagon of food and things set up and is making money hand over fist by selling the things at such outlandish prices. Even if he is a Finn, he is a good man, by golly. He will let one of us stay there by his wagon like we are one of his people standing guard. From there we can see into the tent of that phony parson and know if he leaves to go some place.'

Details of the plan were quickly finalized and the teams selected for the first shift of duty. Those not on duty were once again adjured to stay in the camp site, secluded from the bustle of the mining camp, distanced from accidental notice of any member of the gang. All understood they were destined for a time of expectant boredom. As one, they hoped that that time was short.

# CHAPTER 19

Most of life, it seems, consists of periods of routine, even boredom, punctuated occasionally by sudden, brief moments of joy and pleasure, or sadness and heartache, or abrupt and grave danger.

Dwight and Belinda, together with Frank Singler, were fulfilling their shift at the lookout spot Val had established. It was a cluster of boulders at the base of a long hogback that ranged downward from a tall butte. A quarter of a mile away, clearly visible from where they watched, a shallow draw was sparsely populated with scrub cedar, a scraggly pine tree that grew crookedly from the side of the draw, and one large cottonwood tree. Small patches of varying kinds of brush sprouted up from the nearly grassless floor of the wide swale.

Along the far edge of the draw half a dozen patches of rock jutted above the surrounding brush, some with boulders nearly as large as the cluster at their lookout post.

The shifts seemed interminably long. Silence was

essential, so they could not talk. They dared not even move more than necessary, lest they be spotted by some member of the gang coming out to check on the security of the location.

That had happened often enough to convince all of the posse that this was, in fact, where the gold was hidden. None of the gang had been foolish enough actually to check it, however. Every one who appeared had only studied the ground for evidence of anyone else disturbing the site, then had ridden away again.

This was the third time their particular trio had manned the lookout. Deer flies bedeviled them almost constantly. They buzzed around their faces, landed on any exposed skin, and bit if they were not shooed off instantly. They didn't dare swat one, lest the inevitable noise sound a warning to someone approaching.

Their horses, hidden over a low ridge behind them, stamped and snorted from time to time, badgered by the same pestering insects.

At times a small swarm of gnats would target one or another of the trio. Swarming in front of that person's face, they made remaining still and silent almost impossible. Thirst returned within minutes after every sip from the warm water of a canteen. Time dragged slowly by, inviting carelessness.

Nearly halfway through their shift Belinda's head snapped up. 'Someone's coming,' she breathed.

Dwight and Frank looked at each other, then at Belinda. Neither had heard anything. Belinda held up two fingers. 'Two horses.'

Frowning, Dwight closed his eyes and lowered his head, listening intently. In seconds he heard a hoof click against a stone. The sound came from the direction of the mining camp.

About the same time Frank picked up a sound as well. They crouched down lower, making sure they were not visible to the approaching riders.

In minutes Walt Tighson and Jesse Wrigley rode into view. Obviously watching all around, they rode to the big cottonwood and dismounted. 'Looks like we're the first ones here,' Walt observed.

Jesse fished a watch from his vest pocket, opened the cover, looked at it, snapped it shut and put it back in his vest pocket. 'The rest'll show up right shortly,' he assured.

The trio in the boulders looked at each other with wide-eyed and growing excitement. Dwight silently mouthed to Belinda, 'Go get the others. It's time!'

Wordlessly she nodded. Remaining crouched low enough to be sure that she couldn't be seen from the outlaws' location, she crept around the end of the ridge behind which their horses were tethered. She untied her horse and led him, carefully avoiding any rocks that would make enough sound to betray her, until she was well away from the others. Then she stepped into the saddle and followed the path they had carefully selected for a fast ride to summon the rest of the posse.

She adjudged herself far enough to be out of sound's range, and had started to kick her horse to a gallop when a rider appeared squarely in her path. A raspy voice stopped her cold.

'Now would you look at who thinks she's going to play Paul Revere!'

She gasped, jerking her horse to a stop. Jarvis McCrae sat his horse, blocking her path. He grinned wickedly at her. 'We meet again,' he gloated.

In spite of the grin, which she could only describe as 'nasty', he looked terrible. His sallow cheeks were sunken. His eyes were heavily shadowed, with dark bags beneath them. He had several days' stubble. His hair, jutting from beneath his hat, was matted and tangled. His shirt hung on his shoulders as if it were two sizes too big for his frame.

Before Belinda could react he reached out and grasped the reins of her horse. Jerking them out of her hand, he swayed slightly in the saddle, then recovered his balance. 'Thought you was bein' real smart, didn't you? I spotted you yesterday, so I've been watching to see what you and that no-good marshal sweetheart of yours were up to. Now let me guess. They've figured out that everybody's on their way to meet out here, so your job is to hurry back and get whoever else is waiting, right?'

Her eyes, wide with fear, darted this way and that. When she failed to answer, he said, 'I thought so. Well, sweetheart, I'll tell you what Mac and Belinda are going to do. We're going to go to a spot I've got all figured out, where we can watch that marshal of yours get himself killed thinking he has help coming that won't show up, then you and me are going to take my share of that money and ride off into the sunset together. Unless, of course, you try to do something stupid like running or yelling or something. Then you're going to die real sudden, and I'll have to ride off into the sunset all by myself.'

She knew with terrifying certainty that he was being totally honest. He had the reins of her horse. She could bail out of the saddle and run for it, but he would shoot her in the back without a second thought. If she let him lead her to the vantage point he obviously had already selected, she would be forced to watch the man she loved fail, because of her. He and Frank would wait as long as they could, then they would confront the gang, certain that she was bringing help. When that help didn't come, desperately outnumbered they would certainly be killed.

Despair washed over her. This time not even Dwight would be riding to her rescue. He would die with the rest. She was all alone. There was no way out.

# CHAPTER 20

'Most of 'em are here.'

'Yeah, an' Belinda ain't had time to get the rest.'

'Let's hope whatever they got cookin' is gonna take a while.'

Dwight and Frank spoke in soft whispers, even though a stiff breeze was blowing toward them. That breeze carried the outlaws' voices clearly to them, but would have made it all but impossible for their own words to be overheard. They had been watching the activity as members of the outlaw gang assembled near the big cottonwood.

'Someone's comin',' Dwight hissed.

He and Val crouched amongst the boulders, trying desperately to remain both silent and hidden, but hidden now from both directions. The soft scuffing of shoe soles on boulders grew closer.

'Are you fellows there?'

Relief erupted explosively from both Dwight and Frank. 'That you, Val?'

'Yes,' the voice said.

In seconds, the round top of Lindquist's derby appeared, followed seconds later by the rest of his face. 'Are they here yet?' he asked in that same soft whisper.

'Most of 'em,' Dwight affirmed. 'Seven, by my count.'

'Who is still missing?'

'McCrae.'

'He may have died,' Val suggested. 'Either that or he's unable to join the rest. I spotted him yesterday, and he looked awfully peaked.'

'I thought I hit 'im at least once,' Dwight affirmed.

'Has the wagon showed up yet?'

Dwight and Frank looked at each other, then back at the Pinkerton detective. 'What wagon?' Frank whispered.

'The one they plan to haul the gold out of here in,' Val informed them. 'I've been watching the road coming from Headland, on a hunch. Today it paid off. I also know who the mastermind is, and he is coming after the gold.'

Silence and suspense dangled together in the still air. Both men stared at Val, waiting for an explanation that he was in no hurry to give. Relishing their confusion and curiosity, he eased over to the spot amongst the boulders from which he could see the assembled outlaws.

'It looks like they're getting a poker game together,' he whispered.

Frank and Dwight put their curiosity on hold long enough to join him and confirm his guess. The

150

outlaws had spread a blanket on the ground. They were all seated on it, and one was shuffling a deck of cards.

The three eased back to a more secure spot. 'What are they doin'?' Frank pondered.

'Waiting.'

'For what?'

'For the wagon. They seem to know it's coming today, but not how soon.'

'They ain't made any effort to dig up the gold, or whatever they need to do,' Dwight observed.

'Let's move farther away,' Frank urged, fearful that a sudden change of breeze would betray their presence to the outlaws.

They moved cautiously back over the low ridge to where Val had left his horse. Then both men silently faced Lindquist, awaiting his explanation.

As usual, the Pinkerton man sounded almost like a teacher lecturing his class. The impression always irritated Dwight, but he held his peace, waiting for the explanation. 'They are not likely to do that until the wagon actually arrives. They wouldn't want to have to abandon the location in a hurry with all that gold exposed. It is much too heavy to hide again in a hurry, should they need to do so.'

'Makes sense,' Dwight admitted.

'So who is it who's coming?' Frank demanded.

Val grinned, obviously relishing his role. 'Well, think about it,' he lectured. 'Whoever is behind this operation must be someone with both the ability to dispose of a massive amount of gold, and also an

151

insider's knowledge of the best time to launch a foray to purloin it.'

'To do what?' Frank demanded with a frown.

'To poach it. Pilfer it. Steal it.'

'Oh.'

'So knock off the riddles and tell us who it is, before I get tired of your game and wrap a gun barrel over your head,' Dwight threatened.

Val's grin widened. 'Sorry about that,' he lied. 'Couldn't resist a bit of teasing. The man I saw driving a wagon this way is none other than Hiram Birdwell.'

Both men gasped. 'The banker?' Frank said.

'The same,' Val said. 'It almost had to be him. He handles nearly all the gold coming from the mines, so it would be a simple matter for him to form a fictitious mining company, include the gold from that company with the other shipments, and collect all the revenues accruing to it. He would become independently wealthy, with nobody ever any the wiser. Anybody my agency sent to investigate would waste all their time and effort searching for a huge cache of gold that would be securely in his vault the whole time, shipped out little by little.'

'We'd best get back an' keep our eyes peeled,' Dwight ordered. He didn't know why the cocksureness of the detective nettled him so much, but he had to keep a tight rein on his anger whenever they spent any amount of time talking.

They were scarcely in place again when one of the outlaws jerked his head up. He moved swiftly and gracefully to his feet, the poker game forgotten. 'Someone's comin',' he said quietly.

Nobody argued. Every man rose to his feet. Some moved away to positions of less exposure. Every man among them had a gun in his hand.

The watchers heard the sounds as clearly as the outlaws had. The creaking and rattling of a wagon approached from the east. 'I believe the gentleman has arrived,' Val whispered.

In minutes a wagon appeared, with Hiram Birdwell perched on the driver's seat. Beside him sat one of the guards from the bank.

'He brought a guard,' Frank breathed. 'That's Slim Jenkins.'

'I would wager two to one that a tragic accident is planned for Mr Jenkins before that gold gets back to Headland,' Val guessed. 'That way nobody alive will know that he has it.'

A sudden flurry of activity gripped the assembled outlaws. Grabbing shovels that none of the three watchers had seen, they hurried to a large boulder some twenty-five feet from the cottonwood tree. Digging swiftly, they uncovered the cache of gold in minutes and began carrying it to the wagon. It took less than half an hour for it to be loaded.

As it was, Birdwell stood beside the wagon. He placed a pistol on the wagon seat, just beside where he stood. He also carried a double-barreled shotgun, cradled loosely in his right arm.

His guard, Slim Jenkins, also carried a shotgun, and wore two pistols. He stood behind the banker, with his back to him, so that it was impossible for anyone to approach from any direction without being in clear view of one or the other.

'Takin' no chances,' Frank offered quietly.

When the gold was loaded the outlaws lined up as if they were waiting to see a sideshow at a circus. To each man Birdwell handed a bundle of paper money. To a man, each stayed where he stood until he had counted it, then nodded and moved off.

'Where's them other guys?' Frank worried. 'We ain't got much time. They're gonna start headin' out any minute.'

'We seem to be one man short,' Birdwell announced.

'Who cares?' one of the outlaws said. 'I'm outa here.'

Dwight noticed for the first time that Val carried the Colt revolving shotgun that he had shown him earlier in town. His own forty five was in his hand, as was Frank's in his.

'We have to move now,' Val said, stepping out from behind the boulders.

Swiftly Dwight and Frank ranged a few steps to either side of him. It took several seconds for the outlaws to spot them. Just as one of them did, and swore, Val yelled, 'Throw up your hands, all of you! You are all under arrest.'

Before the swiftest among them could get his gun clear of its leather, another voice bellowed, 'Hold it right there! Nobody is arresting anybody!'

All eyes swivelled to the new voice. Jarvis McCrae

walked into the clearing, shoving Belinda ahead of him, one hand gripping the back of her dress, his gun in his other hand. 'Hey, Marshal,' Mac's voice jeered, 'it seems like we've done this once already.'

Dwight swore helplessly.

Mac laughed, relishing the moment. 'It sure is nice of you to supply us a ticket out of here, Marshal,' he taunted.

He turned his attention momentarily to Birdwell. 'I'll be taking my cut now too, banker. Just toss it on the ground there.'

Belinda's eyes were glued on Dwight as if trying to send him some silent message. The signal was not lost on Dwight. 'Drop!' he yelled.

The instant he yelled, his gun leaped from its holster into his hand. Belinda collapsed as if she had suddenly fainted. His hand still locked on the back of her dress, Mac was jerked slightly off balance. Dwight's gun roared. Whatever was in Mac's mind flew from the back of his skull, along with his life.

Almost as one with the roar of Dwight's forty-five, the first round bellowed from the barrel of the revolving shotgun in the hands of the Pinkerton detective. Its roar swallowed up the slightly less powerful report of Frank's forty-four.

Six shotgun blasts and nine rounds from two handguns were answered by close to a dozen frantic shots from the outlaws' guns. The air was alive with whizzing bullets and buckshot, curses and screams, and the neighing of panicked horses, fighting against harnesses tethering them to a heavy wagon

155

with its brakes firmly set.

Then there was silence. Sudden, utter, overwhelming, breathless silence. Belinda lifted her face from where she had buried it against the ground. She saw the Pinkerton detective, the empty revolving shotgun at his feet, pistol in hand, looking around, watching for any sign of life from any of the outlaws.

Beside him, Frank Singler lay on the ground. His head was up, and his gun was in his hand. His other hand gripped his lower leg. Blood trickled from the side of his head.

Dwight was nowhere in sight. She jerked her eyes around frantically. Beside her the eyes of Hiram Birdwell stared sightlessly up from the ground at her. She jerked away from him, springing to her feet with a startled squeal, and whirled to look behind her.

She saw Mac and Dwight at almost the same instant. Mercifully, Mac was lying on his back, so it was only the front of his face that showed. Just below the left eye a round black hole bore witness to the deadly aim of the man who had once again rescued her.

Then her eyes focused on Dwight. His left arm dangled at his side, blood dripping from the ends of his fingers. His forty-five was in his right hand. She realized suddenly that she hadn't seen him because he was standing directly over her, protectively, watching for any further threats.

'You OK, Frank?' Dwight asked.

'I'm OK,' Frank lied. 'Took one in the leg, but I don't think it's all that bad.'

'Lost a nick outa one ear, too, it looks like,' Dwight observed.

Frank lifted a hand to his head, then studied the blood smeared across his palm. 'That's gettin' a mite close,' he observed.

'You OK, Lindquist?'

'Quite well, yes, thank you,' Val replied, sounding as if he were sitting in a parlor visiting with friends.

'You handle that big shotgun like nothin' I ever seen,' Dwight marveled.

'It fires quite rapidly, doesn't it,' Val agreed. 'It requires great concentration to keep it moving as rapidly as one tends to squeeze the trigger.'

Dwight couldn't keep the awe from his voice. 'They was all too surprised to move, for a couple o' seconds. Then it looked like grain gettin' mowed down with a sickle,' he said. 'I run outa anyone to shoot at afore I hardly got started.'

'Honey! You're hurt!' Belinda realized suddenly.

'Just nicked a bit,' Dwight dismissed her concern.

All four whirled at the sound of running horses approaching. The three members of the posse who were due to relieve Dwight, Val and Belinda thundered up the draw, guns drawn, obviously responding to the fusillade of gunfire.

They reined in their horses in a cloud of dust, eyes jerking here and there, finally realizing it was all over.

Belinda tore her eyes from them and looked once more at the dead outlaw who had used her as a hostage. She knew full well he had intended to use her for much more than that. She shuddered as she

157

looked at his sightless eyes. She refused to look away. She wanted more than almost anything in that moment to be totally sure she need never fear him again.

# EPILOGUE

They didn't really think they needed to defend the cargo. After all, it appeared to be only a wagon, too heavily laden with dead bodies. Visibly it was a veritable flood of business for the undertaker, Cornelius Janderslaag, when they got back to Headland. Even so, the members of the posse ranged protectively before and behind the wagon the whole way.

With what had been loaded on to Belinda's horse, all the stolen gold had been recovered. It lay incognito beneath the macabre load of death, en route back to its owners.

Nearly all the paper money was recovered as well, all packed into the outlaws' pockets, bedrolls and saddle-bags. Along with it was the considerable amount of paper money that Birdwell had brought with him to pay off the members of the gang. Because of that added cash, the posse brought considerably more back into Headland than the outlaws had taken out of it. The excess amount was divided between the widows of the men killed in the robbery.

It wouldn't replace their lost husbands, but it would provide them with a comfortable living for a goodly while.

The wedding was a quiet, modest affair, in the pastor's parlor in Headland. The pastor's wife and Val Lindquist served as witnesses. Both bride and groom, his left arm still bandaged, wanted only to have some private and quiet time together. Maybe fifty years or so, for starters, Dwight figured.